LILY
OF THE
VALLEY

MEG DAVIS

Published in North America, Australia, and Europe by RIZE.
Visit Running Wild Press at www.runningwildpublishing.
com/rize. Educators, librarians, book clubs (as well as the
eternally curious), go to www.runningwildpublishing.com/rize.

ISBN (pbk) 978-1-963869-51-4
ISBN (ebook) 978-1-963869-56-9

To my dog, without whom I truly would not have been here to have written this book. You saved me. I can't wait to read this to you.

CONTENTS

"WHAT DO A STALKER AND a Vestal want in these parts?" The gatekeeper standing guard at a massive, hoisted portcullis, the ingress into the city, jeered down the end of his pointed poleaxe. The Stalker noted that the tip of the weapon was not even sharp but was rather an accoutrement of ceremonial ornamentation meant to frighten away dullards and beggars. "Your kind aren't welcome here in Gundrada. Neither of you," he grunted.

"Is your Temple just for show then?" The Stalker took a step toward the portcullis noting also that the gears had lingered open for a long time on account of a thick skin of rust. *This town has always been a rotting shithole.* He kicked a small stone from beneath his boot at the guard's armour which had long ago lost its lustre. "Anyway, I'm here by request: Rathar of Borghild to serve a Master Orien," the Stalker growled. "She comes with me, obviously." Rathar gestured to Gisela, his counterpart, who stood motionless in the shadow of the portcullis.

"Orien hired you? Vagabond filth?" The leather vambraces on his arms quivered as he held his ceremonial poleaxe out, his voice the bravest thing about him. Rathar sighed and produced from his pocket a piece of parchment detailing, in short, the local magician's summons for his *expertise*. It was signed with an official Consortium seal.

"Orien don't need your help," the guardsman's voice began to quaver. "O-Orien can handle the beast without the likes of you."

"That's not what the warlock surmises, and never has that been the case in the history of all the Provinces." Rathar grasped the guardsman's neck with one strong arm and pinned him against the wall framing the decaying portcullis, poleaxe falling to the ground with an unceremonious clank. "Which way?"

"Rathar," the Vestal's clear voice was like a song.

"The north tower," the guardsman choked, his fear quickly getting the better of him.

The Stalker turned to his companion and grimaced, "You're supposed to get me into places, Sela, not keep me out of them."

"Let him go, Rathar. The Provinces change swifter than the wind."

"Apparently so. Suddenly I'm at the beck and call of *magicians*." Rathar rolled his eyes and dropped the guardsman to the ground along with the crumpled summons, and they proceeded into the city under the veil of darkness.

"Go and find somewhere for us to lodge tonight. Off the main road," Rathar rasped, pulling the leather strap of his cloak more snuggly to his brawny shoulders.

"You know," Gisela reached in the dark for Rathar's arm as he was already walking away, "it's illegal for a Stalker to be without a Vestal in these parts."

"Do as I say. I don't need you anyway. What I do need is to gather some information on Orien; I'd never simply walk up to a magician under these circumstances. Don't worry, I'll keep to the shadows."

I don't need you anyway. The words stung like a blackthorn prick, but Gisela nodded and did as she was told. "God is with you." Gisela sighed as Rathar vanished into the darkness of the overcrowded, dirty buildings. She was always wary when Rathar went out on his own; except for very rare places of particular jurisdiction, usually in the open country and unmarked roads where the endless plains met the mountaintops, it was illegal for Stalkers to travel without Vestals to influence them. Stalkers were powerful beings, with potent abilities and a nature to kill. They kept whole Provinces and races safe from the aspirmeyg beasts that wreaked havoc on the Provinces, but their wills could be weak. Stalkers had no moral compass, nothing to tell them when to stop killing, and sometimes the thirst could not be quenched. At the Abbey, Gisela had heard terrible tales of Stalkers who had killed aspirmeygs and in turn, throngs of innocents afterward in plain and simple bloodlust. This is why every Stalker was required to travel with a Vestal companion, a spiritual guide who exercised a moral compass and influence over the Stalker. The Vestal controlled the thirst, and the Stalker was not put to death, but rather put to work. Rathar and Gisela had been a team for many years, yet there was no doubt that there was something very different about Rathar than that which afflicted other Stalkers.

It was not until late that Rathar returned to the spot he had left Gisela.

"The moon is high; where have you been? I was worried."

"That I had been caught? No, you weren't. You ought to know me better than that."

"They are not welcoming of our kind here, Rath. Orien will not likely have told anyone that he hired you."

"Did you find somewhere?" Rathar ignored Gisela's fussing as he often did; he found that when travelling in the company of women it was most endurable to hear what one wanted to hear and no more.

"The Temple is locked. It seems they really are suspicious of us here, and no inn will take a Stalker certainly, but there is an old stable unused down that road a ways, tucked behind a row of willow trees. That should be cover enough." Gisela pulled his hood up. "You stick out like a sore thumb in this filth; best no one sees you." She cocked her head in a manner that said *do as I say and come along now,* which Rathar did just so, indulgently or at least not voicing any complaints.

When they arrived at the stable, they laid out their cloaks for sleep atop the old, dry straw and ancient manure. Rathar sat staring out into the darkness.

"You cannot sit up another night. Even you must sleep."

"Someone could appear out of this wretched gloom."

"That is not your true worry." Gisela moved her cloak beside Rathar and sat down. They looked out into the grungy obscurity of Gundrada, damp thatched rooves covering soot-stained bricks so close together you couldn't escape the disheartening sounds of life in poverty, nor the moans that bandaged them for a while, nor the wails of the hungry, bastard children that came soon after that.

"You were right. Orien hasn't told a soul." Rathar sparked a bit of flint over a whittled, red pipe and began to puff. "There is an aspirmeyg beast lurking near here, but everyone seems to think that Orien has it under control, that he can quell it or wield it in some way. I don't know a magician alive that could kill an aspirmeyg. He has these paupers in the palm of his hand, but for what?"

"What do we even know about Orien?"

"He's the magician benefiting this duchy, though I couldn't say how, look at this place." Rathar scoffed. "And we've heard his name from the Consortium before; he leads them, so he has power."

"And the beast?"

"For all the stock they put in Orien, you think they wouldn't be so fearful, but they are. The people are terrified. It comes every three nights to feed, they say, like clockwork. Those are the only whispers I heard."

"You know the lore of all aspirmeygs, surely you know. What kind does that?"

"An aspirmeyg on a schedule?" Rathar let his mouth fall open. "I don't know everything." He stared into the darkness for a while and ran his palms over his eyes through the haze of tussocky smoke. Gisela could see his weariness glaze over him like a steady rain; she knew his desire to speak was waning.

"God has revealed many things to me, Rathar. He shows me your burdens." Rathar said nothing. "You do not carry them alone." Gisela paused and looked at the strong frame beside her. "It has been a long time since you were under my influence as a Vestal. You act freely. I am nothing more than a formality to you." She frowned.

"You're a friend." He scowled and grated the bit of his pipe between his teeth.

"A friend, then. As a friend, trust me when I say that you can trust yourself, Rathar. You're no ordinary Stalker. Back at the Abbey you know they call us 'The Chosen Pair.' It's our duty to look at these signs. To notice prophec—"

"Sela. You know I am not keen to speak about this."

"Now sleep," she whispered and put her warm hand on the base of Rathar's neck. A consuming weight overcame him, and he felt his eyes grow suddenly very heavy; sleep was compassing him in a way he could not curb, like honeybees in summer circling and groping the linden trees. Very soon he fell over into a dormant heap. "I will sit up and watch tonight." She smiled, brushing his earthy, red hair away from his face, and carefully placing aside the wooden pipe, inhaling the rich aroma as she tapped out the ashes, almost, she thought, a sort of vice.

•• ———— ••●•• ———— ••

Morning came as the sun had just begun to show its rays, and a delicate frost covered the ground in a glistening white gossamer. Rathar squinted into the dingy light and pulled his cloak closer around him.

"Don't be lazy." Gisela's voice was like a song piercing the silence of the ill-lit morning. "If we want to reach the north tower without attracting attention, it's best to travel before true morning."

"I'm not supposed to be asleep. . ." Rathar stumbled to stand. He rubbed his blurry eyes awake. "Why do you do this to me?" Rathar had always found this little trick of Gisela's particularly maddening in the same breath as it was refreshing. He hadn't slept like that in a spell.

"No time to point fingers." Gisela placed two yellow-fleshed apples in his hands. While the people slept, there was a heaviness in the air in the streets of Gundrada, though, Rathar thought, it may have just been the excessive smell of putrid food and excrement dumped in the gutters that hung about obnoxiously at nose level. When they reached the north tower, it stood, a striking naked spire against smooth stone without any protrusions. Orien obviously had an air of confidence in the sleepy town. "It stinks; can you smell it?" Rathar asked.

"Of what?" Gisela's grey eyes darted around, checking her surroundings.

"Fear." He chuckled, and slowly, like a poison seeping through his ashen skin and creeping along his body the shift began. It looked utterly horrible, grotesque even; that's what Gisela had thought the first time she'd seen it. Rathar looked like his very body was burning as a fleshy claret began to colour him like a terrible wound.

"Relax, Rathar, you're nowhere near the beast, and you're already shifting. He breathed deeply through his nose and grinned, looking almost beastly himself.

"Doesn't hurt to be prepared against a reputation like Orien's. He's head of the damned magician's Consortium. We don't know what to expect." They approached the north tower and entered with little dispute from the duke's crudely plated guards; they were expected. Before them was a staircase lit by cast-iron sconces bearing torches. Gisela took a torch out of the heavy rest and led the way up the winding, damp stairway that seemed endless wherein the steps were so small her big toes pressed together and Rathar's shoulders shuffled against the stone walls. Surely the light was growing outside as they climbed on. When at last they reached the end, they came to a large, iron fettered door. It was tall but unassuming, not at all what Gisela expected of the head of the Consortium. Rathar's breath was rattling. Gisela looked him in the eyes, "Orien is the head of the Consortium, Rathar. Relax, I beg you. A disorderly blunder here could have consequences." She turned and reached her hand to the door, but before she could knock there was a hollow sounding voice.

"Enter the Stalker and his overseer." Gisela winced at Orien's words. Rathar didn't take kindly to slights, especially from the lips of magicians with whom he held a permanent and rather callow grudge. The door opened wide into a curious, round room filled with old books laid open and dusted over, bottles and glass orbs filled with all colours and draughts, and in the middle atop a magnificent wooden throne with red, velvet, moth-eaten cushions sat Orien, Gundrada's magical benefactor.

"Stalker, welcome." Orien remained stiff in a powerful posture, his wrinkled hands grasping his knees confidently and surprisingly, his face remained youthful and bright, beset with sparkling blue eyes and thin pursed lips.

"Am I welcome here?" Rathar laughed. Gisela's eyes flitted from Rathar to Orien.

"And what, Stalker, makes you think otherwise? I have invited you, have I not? I sought out your specialist services."

"The duke himself knows not that I am here." Orien shifted in his seat ever so slightly uncomfortably, something Rathar was keen to notice and eager to take advantage of.

"And," Rathar kicked the debris from his boots onto a heap of books on the floor, "I slept in shit last night."

"The duke has many cares. Too many to deal with *my* matters."

"Humble lodgings for the head of the Consortium wouldn't you say? Usually your kind reek of excess." Rathar looked around, his voice dripping with mockery.

"I am a humble man," Orien replied seriously.

"You do reek of fear though." In the blink of an eye, Rathar was gone from the entry of the great door and was before Orien's throne with one great, pale hand spread across his chest. "It must be a dreadful aspirmeyg." Rathar's hand was crushing Orien's ribs, making it difficult to breathe.

"Vestal," Orien's voice just barely wavered but betrayed no weakness, "command this Stalker to release me at once."

"Rathar, we are here for a purpose." Gisela's voice was firm. "I apologise," she looked softly at Orien as Rathar released him. "Stalkers do enjoy the smell of fear." Orien pursed his lips.

"This beast is immune to my magic. I cannot destroy it."

"What do you mean? It is common knowledge that aspirmeygs cannot be vanquished by magic. Why do the people of Gundrada have such confidence in you? We were not welcome here from the moment we arrived. Surely, the people would praise a Stalker in times such as these," Gisela pressed gently.

"It was never meant to escape! How it got out, I do not know."

"Got out?" Rathar snarled.

"A Boreas." Orien sighed. "There was a Boreas, weakened. . . almost dead on my travels past. I had been experimenting with a bit of magic, and I thought surely I could hold the beast with my magical prison. . . what if. . . what if with this new magic, we could match the power of Stalkers, surpass them even?"

"This magic. . ." Rathar glared.

"It needs refining, of course. The Boreas escaped somehow. Every three nights it hunts the people of this town. I cannot stop it. By the castle it comes."

A low growl came from Rathar's throat.

"Fascinating." Orien leaned forward in his seat admiring the sinewy flesh that had grown over Rathar's eyes and the claret bruises that dappled his skin. Rathar inhaled through his nose and noticed that the scent of fear was diminished and replaced with. . . madness. "The Stalker's affliction they call it."

"It is what we call shifting, sir. For some say it takes a beast to kill a beast." Gisela said. Rathar smirked, and in a blink, he had vanished through the tower window, skidding partway down the unclad tower and lunging from it forcefully into the tall oaks skirting the greensward.

•• ———— ••●•• ———— ••

In the shadow of the castle's curtain wall, Rathar waited, heart beating stolidly, bronze gimlet knives wedged between his fingers, jutting out past his knuckles. He could not see, having shifted with his eyes grown over, but he could smell everything, and it painted a map around him better than eyes ever could. As the sun rose high, he waited for the Boreas; there were four types of aspirmeygs, each as hideous as the next. Boreas were aspirmeygs which manipulated stone, Zephyrs licking flames, Notos harnessed the cruel power of ice and chill, and Eurus torrents of violent water. They did not all travel or live together, rather they dwelt and travelled alone and kept to certain regions of the Provinces, but aspirmeygs were deadly to all races, in any of their types, except for Stalkers. They could be seen, but in battle it was as if the conflict was a poison dream for they had no tangible form; no weapon could strike them, nor spell could bind them, but their wisping bodies were as venom against a man so that he burned or drowned to death or so that he was crushed by a stone that was not there; however, against a Stalker, aspirmeygs were suddenly corporeal and material. Against a Stalker, aspirmeygs were vulnerable.

The scent came to Rathar and a frenzied hunger drew the image before him. Out from the forest and toward the castle came a beast, massive and muscular with long sharp claws dragging along the ground and a face cruel but not unlike the muzzle of a cur with fangs and foam speckling its growling lips. To anyone else the creature would have seemed pale and wispy like it was made of cloudstuff, but to Rathar the beast was there in ugly candour; he could sense its heinous form curled over itself in the pale dim of morning. Rathar's body was as if under a spell, the desire to kill surging within him. He lunged toward the Boreas with his blades outstretched and narrowly missed the jab of the goliath claws. The Boreas was in a fury, not having expected an adversary but rather an easy meal, piercing the earth all around him. The creature was moderately fast, but Rathar was faster, moving in a blink from place to place, predicting the beast's every move by the stink of it. It was slow and weakened somehow. Standing still for a moment, baiting the Boreas, he drew from his side the shining, bronze sabre that rested there and powerfully swung up as the Boreas descended upon him with a wisping, mammoth stone that it seemed to have conjured up from nowhere, slashing at the throat of the manged, sawtoothed head that descended upon him from above. That should have been the end of it, but miraculously the Boreas still had a spark inside. Its blood spilled down its body still, and it swung its massive claws around toward Rathar in fury. He ducked smoothly and impaled the beast through the tender flesh of its armpit down into the heart and watched as the claws crumple to the ground while dark, purple blood spilled, welling around his boots. There was a small part of him that desired more; to rip and tear, to hear ligaments snap and blood spatter, but he drew his thoughts elsewhere and quelled the urge. His Vestal. Where was Gisela? The thrill of blood pulsed within him. He squeezed his eyes tightly. He needed to go back to the north tower. Rathar inhaled the stink of the beast upon the ground, it was a ripe scent that carried with it the simple pleasures of life for a Stalker, rancid and lustfully familiar. With one monstrous plunge, he ripped the heart out of its chest.

•• ——— ••●•• ——— ••

"Rathar!" Gisela turned to him as he entered the north tower and chucked the heart before Orien in a splash of wisping plumes of purple. "Shifting back is always the hardest," Gisela whispered and gently pressed her two thumbs over Rathar's calloused eyes. His hands, dyed amaranthine, grasped her wrists as the knotty sinews over his eyes slowly retreated. "You have done what we came here for. The people of Gundrada are safe," Gisela spoke softly.

"No." Rathar grunted and staggered towards Orien, shooting a glare at him with one eye untethered. "You let the Boreas go on purpose." Gisela grabbed for Rathar, but he pushed her away with a discreet carefulness that she noticed. Orien did not seem to notice; he backed slowly against his seat. "People have been talking." Rathar picked up Orien by the collar of his tunic, and his feet dangled above the ground. "The duke has been away from the castle, Orien."

"H. . . has. . . he?" Orien stuttered, grasping at the muscular hand holding him swaying in the air.

"I hear he's been providing for the peasants personally from his stores with winter looming, millet and the like. The man has a warm heart and is in favour with the people. Is that a favour you wish to relish?" Rathar pulled Orien close. "You just can't control its hunger, its target. It comes by the castle, but you haven't been able to come near enough. It's the duke you want, isn't it, for some petty squabble? That's the aim of your magic. Court politics not to your fancy in this shithole?"

"You're not implying that I. . . that I would. . . " Orien choked at the tightening of his ruff.

"You tell me."

"Rathar," Gisela touched his shoulder, "we are not here for politics. We came for the beast, and that we accomplished." She was surprised and a little embarrassed by his outburst. Rathar didn't hide the fact that he didn't fancy magicians, save the one that raised him for whom he held a place of utmost respect in his heart, but unlike his Stalker brethren, Rathar usually held himself with a bit *more* propriety. Orien stayed in a heap where Rathar dropped him.

"Rathar." Gisela held out her hand, and he took it, slowly returning to the strong, snow-white figure he most often showed.

"Take your Boreas." Rathar kicked the purple, wisping heart toward Orien and scooped a handful of silver coins from the long table beside him into his purse, "And I'll take my pay from your pocket seeing as you locked your Temple to keep your precious reputation." With that he and Gisela strode back toward the winding stair, but Orien called after them.

"Think of what we could accomplish without you brutes, Rathar." Rathar disliked the way his name slithered off of Orien's tongue with ill-intent. "In shitholes like this, as you so delicately put it, where people have no hope, a malady which I hope to finally extinguish once and for all from this grotty backwater, and barely a confidence in a God, they need to cling to *powerful people* Rathar, magic and those who can wield it. Magicians are the noble past and they are the judicious way forward."

"Is that why you summoned me to clean up your mess?" Rathar shouted and jingled his silver proudly.

"I will perfect my magic," Orien whispered. As they left, Rathar saw in a piece of shining crystal hanging on the wall above the stair, the reflection of Orien, smiling smugly at their backs. He grinned himself.

Chapter

02

T HE SUN HUNG HIGH IN the sky and beat down
with warm, lazy rays on the fading grass below. Rathar
lay with his eyes closed, letting the warmth touch
his alabaster face. Gisela sat beside him watching his features
unmoving as stone.

"Rathar."

"Mmm."

"Back in Gundrada. . ."

"Mmm."

"You weren't under my influence, you know."

"Mmm."

"Rathar." This time nothing. She reached over and hovered her hand over his face.

"The only tepid day in weeks, don't steal that away from me." He pushed her hand aside without opening his eyes.

"Then talk to me."

"Women always want to talk." Rathar rolled over onto his stomach, letting the sun cover his back and shoulders, seeping through the holes in his tattered tunic. "They ought to have men as Vestals. I'd have some peace and quiet," he chuckled to himself, and Gisela smiled. In truth, the sound of Gisela's voice was no bothersome thing at all; after the many years they had spent as companions, navigating the Provinces many times over, Rathar had grown used to, even comforted by the warble of the Vestal.

"I know you lied about Orien setting the Boreas after the duke. I know you well enough to tell." Gisela wagged her finger. "Why did you do it?"

"I wanted Orien to think he had us deluded in a way. He was trying to control an aspirmeyg with magic after all. It seemed there was more to the story, that we'd be safer in the dark for now. You're always safest when you know little about the schemes of magicians." There was a long pause. Rathar turned his head toward Gisela without opening his eyes. "Sela, I got rowdy. But like you say. . ."

"Like I say?"

"Yeah." He turned his head away again.

"Rath."

"I don't want to talk about—"

"No, Rathar, look," Gisela pointed toward a distant speck on the road, "someone is coming this way. What do you see?" Rathar propped himself up onto his elbows and squinted; Stalkers had excellent farsighted vision.

"It's an old man."

"Maybe he is just passing by."

"No. . ." Rathar inhaled deeply. "He smells of purpose." They waited for the man to come up the road by the dell they were resting in, and just as Rathar had predicted, he approached the pair pointedly.

"They said there was a Stalker in these parts, a firestorm for hair, travelling with the loveliest of Vestals." The old man tipped his straw hat, shading him in the sun. "I always thought it was peculiar." The old man leaned over his horse's neck. "A Stalker's skin is paler than a ghost. I wonder why? Is it because you truly are to be feared as phantoms like the wights you come from?"

"And I wonder what brings you to outcasts such as ourselves?" Rathar growled.

"Outcasts from Gundrada to Guise perhaps, but sought out beyond those borders." The old man seemed jolly.

"You seek the services of a Stalker then?" Gisela sang.

"I don't fear your kind, boy," the old man said buoyantly. "I've been looking for you since I heard the Boreas was slain in Gundrada. Something is killing my horses. I run a stable south of Lanthchilde in Bero."

"Have no other Stalkers passed through Bero?" Rathar grunted.

"I have no money, and Bero has no Temple; the Stalker residing in Bero now won't work." Rathar at once caught the old man in his feeble attempt at a lie. A stableman from Bero, a town known for its outsourcing of fine horses, would not be penniless.

"A Temple is not a prerequisite to labour. Stalkers go where there is a need as a general rule, but slake my curiosity, gaffer, what makes you think I will work?"

"Surely, you've heard the rumours about the Stalker who wanders with a Vestal, but needs her for naught. They say, years ago, he defended the burg of Garburh but the bloodlust did not overtake him. They say he's of a noble disposition unlike his barbarous kin if you know what I mean, and I think, young master, you *do* know what I mean. Have I found that Stalker?"

Rathar's eyes flashed from Gisela to the old man. "No payment, no work? That's how this other Stalker teases you so, eh? I don't believe it; and I'm not keen to head to Bero; it stinks of horses."

"Come with me." The old man nodded. "I think you'll find that you will change your mind. . . if you are who I think you are."

"Why should I?"

"What else are you doing?"

"Enjoying the day."

"Stalkers go where there is a need, as a general rule. Are you coming, or aren't you?"

"To Bero," said Gisela. "Lest you lie around and get lazy," she jested. Rathar frowned at her, but they soon found themselves packing up their meager belongings and following the old man down the road.

•• ———— ••●•• ———— ••

The ancient town of Bero was once a place where great dwarven kings ruled over vast stone halls, wondrous to behold. Anymore the dwarves had been driven far from Bero, and men had ruled with a regent for centuries by formality and custom, but the great halls remained and the flags of the dwarven monarchy still rippled in the wind high above the echoing structures. It was a bustling city that busied itself in trading and raising horses.

"Let's stop in for a drink, Stalker. You've been walking for hours."

"I'd rather get to work."

"Don't be a ninny." The old man stepped into a stone tavern, with a door so short one had to duck down, nestled between the foundry and various ateliers. Rathar peered down the road littered with hay and bespeckled with steaming piles of manure and wrinkled his nose.

"What is it?" Gisela tugged on his shirtsleeve.

"Horses." Rathar said. "Useless. Nothing but another mouth to feed." Gisela smiled and pulled Rathar into the Tavern.

"Come, Stalker. Sit down. I'll buy you an ale for your trouble. Some bread and cheese for you and the Vestal." The old man pulled out a few chairs. They sat by lantern light while eating sheep's cheese smeared on rye bread and making polite conversation with tipplers and dwarves of every diversification. Rathar found dwarves to be an exasperating sort, but the ale was stretching his patience and softening his temperament. He was making almost pleasant conversation with a haulier called Crispin, enjoying the pungent smack of the sheep's cheese when they were interrupted by a deep, loud laugh.

"Look who it is, the stableman of Bero." A milky face emerged out of the crowd holding tightly onto two scantily clad women in one large hand and tighter still to two steins in the other. "He's found himself a Stalker for cheap. Tell me, brother, how did he buy you, the penniless horse herder?" The Stalker stumbled forward, obviously drunk and slapped one of the women on her bottom.

"Hardly brothers," Rathar grumbled at the young Stalker, obviously fresh sprang from Borghild.

"We're Stalkers, you and I, raised in the same manner from trug to sword. We're the same."

"You would know then that this man's silver matters naught where your blade is concerned."

"It's Rathar, isn't it? Rathar the red-haired? Winter is on our heels. Temples aren't profitable. I have skills, and I won't throw them away for nothing, Rathar." The Stalker, already large, tried to make himself appear larger.

"You're young and foolish." Rathar sighed. "If profit is what you're after, go lay down your blade at Borghild and seek an occupation as a tax collector or paint portraits for kings; you're not fit to wield it, ignorant prick." Rathar didn't need to look large or intimidating; it came by him naturally, and there was a persecution in his eyes that caused the Stalker to take a few steps backward, though he looked gravely offended. Rathar's savage eyes flickered from the Stalker to Gisela.

"Don't worry. I've got one, too. This old fool would be dead if it weren't for her. I said it once, and I'll say it again. Working for free is insulting." The Stalker spat at the old man and broke into raucous laughter to hide his wounded pride.

"Adel," came a soft, yet determined voice. "That's enough. Leave them alone." The Stalker writhed for a moment, but then settled.

"Fine." He turned toward a slight woman with raven-colored hair and the clothing of a Vestal.

"You see," said the old man approaching Rathar, "I think you're different." Rathar sighed and tipped back his cup quickly and clanked it against the table indicating his need for another.

·· ——— ··●·· ——— ··

It was dark by the time they approached the old man's stable. "Here we are!" he smiled.

"You're optimistic for someone whose livelihood is being massacred by an aspirmeyg."

"Because I have faith in you, Stalker."

"Why's that?" Rathar asked, but he knew the question was footling; the stableman had sized him up accurately.

The old man opened the door to his home, "Because once the horses are gone, it'll come for them." He stretched out his arm and gestured to four, young children huddled around the fire, red cheeked and freckled, each one fatter than necessary, but happy looking.

"What are those?" Rathar growled.

"Those are children."

"I know what. . . I mean. . . why are they here? Aren't you a little old to be fathering children?" Rathar said bluntly.

"These are my grandchildren." The old man laughed and clapped Rathar on the shoulder, evidently finding him to have a sense of humour. "Their parents died of illness some years ago. It's just me and their grandmother to care for them now. Money is tight, running a modest stable and taking care of four children. Tell me Stalker, will you let them die? Do you care so little?"

"Why not take them away?"

"We aren't nomads like you, Stalker. This is all we have. It's all we know. We have nowhere else."

"Rathar." Gisela touched his arm as he looked over to her. "They're just. . ."

"I know."

"So young. . ."

"I know, Sela."

"This is your choice. I won't make it for you." There was a moment of silence.

"Take me to the stable. Leave the Vestal with the children. It's safer that way."

"Thank you," the old man bellowed exaggeratedly.

"Just do it." Rathar stomped his boot which gave the children a fright.

"Yes! Of course! This way! It strikes after sundown. The horses. . . I find them dragged out into the yard. . . with their insides all out."

"Another aspirmeyg on a schedule, and seemingly killing for sport instead of a meal. Peculiar indeed." Rathar pursed his lips and looked around at the vastness of the operation before him. The stable was forty by sixty pens deep, built of great mahogany beams, boasting mares and stallions and colts of the finest variety, glistening coats and tack to befit a duke at least, bits of gold and reins of braided leather, good, strong horses of which he had not seen the likes of except in military parades and knights' jousts.

"A modest stable," Rathar mumbled under his breath, dripping with sarcasm. "Leave me," Rathar rasped. His body began to flood bright red and pink, thick white skin winding and slowly tethering his eyes shut. The old man fled quickly, though brave in the face of Rathar before, to see him shift was an entirely fearful affair. Rathar inhaled deeply, the smell of fear was delicious, and it fueled him.

•• ———— ••●•• ———— ••

The moon rose high in the sky illuminating everything below with a pale smolder. Rathar paced before the stables, listening to the horses step and snort uneasily as he passed. "Come out." He huffed a cloud of white into the autumn air, breathing deeply through his nose, painting the landscape before him with broad strokes and finer until it was laid out before him with such clarity it was as if he was not without his eyes at all but with augmented ones. Suddenly there was a rustle behind; the horses bellowed in alarm, and Rathar saw in the map of his mind behind him a glint of the beast he had been waiting for. Its pungent stench was one he knew well. In a flash, Rathar had jumped from where he stood to the roof of the stable, prowling along the top beam to the back edge on the tips of his toes, but something took him by surprise. The beast was a Zephyr, towering and wrapped in wisping flames; Boreas were living in these parts. . . how could a Zephyr. . . the beast came barreling toward him and hit him in the chest with teeth like razors bared. Both Rathar and the beast landed with a thud onto the ground below, creating a basin in the turf, his jerkin smoking from where it had been singed. With one strong motion,

Rathar pulled the locked jaws of the Zephyr from his heaving chest and pressed his weight into it, tumbling over and pinning it to the ground; he could only maneuver hand to hand with it for so long, however, as even he would become susceptible to the licking of the flames. He reached for the bronze dagger concealed in his boot, but the beast writhed with a powerful threshing and broke free, tearing into the treetops nearby. Rathar climbed to his feet, spinning around. The smell of his own blood was distorting his map. Hastily he wiped his chest with his smoking hands and smelled the air. There it was, in the tree facing south, watching. In one swift movement, Rathar pulled the dagger from its sanctum and with expert calculation cast it straight between the beast's eyes. It slumped to the ground. He made his way, cautiously, toward it and kicked it with his boot several times to make sure it was dead. The Zephyr flinched a little, but without hesitation, and with one motion, the bronze sword from his hip was drawn, and the head of the creature was lopped from its shoulders and rolled a few paces away. Rathar removed his dagger with a little effort from the Zephyr's head; it was blazing hot. He grabbed it with a square of leather from his pocket, wiped it clean, and stowed it along with his sword.

•• ———— ••●•• ———— ••

Gisela was becoming restless and felt that she could wait on Rathar no longer, for there was something about the stableman's home that suffocated her. "I must go out," she exclaimed, surprised at her anxiety. She could simply be of no practical use out of doors, in the face of an aspirmeyg; in fact, Rathar had always made it expressly clear that she was to stay as far away from the dirty work as possible lest she be afflicted by an aspirmeyg's poison touch, but there was a feeling, almost of malice, creeping upon her that she wished to slough.

"Don't you think we should wait for the Stalker to come back?" The old man grasped Gisela's shoulder, uncomfortably close to her neck. She shrugged his hand away for it strangely and eerily burned.

"He is my responsibility," she said, shaking off the feeling. But as the words left her lips the door to the wooden house creaked open, and there stood Rathar, bloodied, still patting out a spark here and there, but standing erect, holding the severed head of a wolf-like creature.

"A Zephyr." Gisela frowned at the gaping scratches on his chest and the scorched skin on his hands.

"Superficial." He ignored her gaze and tossed the head on the floor before the feet of the old man. "Who do you raise horses for?"

"Why?" asked the old man, ushering the children away from the sanguine sight.

"Your stables are vast, your horses good; this is hardly a modest arrangement. And," he added, "Zephyrs don't roam these parts."

"You think. . . the beast has been targeting me?"

"I don't know," Rathar flinched, and Gisela noticed; he had shifted back on his own, a grueling process that had taken nearly two hours without a Vestal to ease the pain and cut the time down to mere minutes. "Strange affairs have been taking place at the hands of magicians. But you're safe for now."

"How can I thank you, Stalker? You've saved my horses, my modest livelihood. . ." Rathar scoffed at the word 'modest' again, yet the old man continued, "the children who are like my very own."

"Food." Rathar grunted, and then glancing down at his injury added, "and a fair bit of comfrey if you have it. We haven't been to the apothecary for a while yet."

"Of course, of course!" The old man took a cloth and wrapped in it assorted fruits and a loaf of bread. Then he rummaged through the cabinets and selected a jar of stinking salve. He pinched his nose and handed it to Gisela who smiled warmly at him. "You're different, Stalker. Different from the others." Rathar said nothing, but kicked the Zephyr's head aside as he walked through the door into the bright light of morning.

"We'll be going now." Rathar said.

"Where is it that you're headed?" the old man asked. Rathar thought it was particularly nosy of him.

"North," he responded as vaguely as possible. "I always find work up there, Notos and the like."

"Good, good," the old man feigned being casual, but Rathar thought he looked awfully like someone who was trying to remember what he had just heard. "But I suggest Lanthchilde. They're generous to your kind there. Your garments are a sore sight, and Lanthchilde has quality merchants to replace such items." Rathar ran his hands, already healing, over the tears in his jerkin and tunic with some consideration.

"May we never meet again, stableman." Rathar motioned for Gisela to follow him.

"On the contrary, Stalker. May we meet under different circumstances." He smiled. Gisela rubbed her neck where it still burned a little.

The cold autumn air seemed to be trapped in the overgrown forest paths. Ferns clung to the trunks of impressive, towering oak trees with a cold dampness. Rathar and Gisela had remained silent for most of the morning apart from the squelch of wet leaves under their boots.

"There will be a fork in the road upcoming." Gisela broke the silence as though lifting a curse.

"What of it?" Rathar snarled. He wasn't in a pleasant mood and up till now, he'd been able to hide it. His last shifting had left him tired, and the Zephyr had left him thinking, and thinking had left him ill-tempered.

"You'll have to decide whether to make our way north or head on to Lanthchilde, but you need something new to wear. Look at yourself; you're all a mess. You can't very well head into winter in tatters."

"That's the least of our worries." He tried not to sound too waspish.

"What do you mean?"

"Orien. . ." Rathar mumbled.

"Orien? What about Orien? You scared him off, and I'd say we're done poking around in the business of magicians, right?" Gisela asked, her pleasant voice piercing the silence of the wood. Rathar said nothing and only continued to walk ahead. Her brow furrowed. "Rath, what are you not telling me?" Rathar sighed heavily and stopped before her. He closed his eyes and breathed deeply through his nose, honing his senses and scanning the area around him.

"No one for an age. Sit down." They both sat balanced on their toes trying to avoid the muck of leaves below, and Rathar leaned in close. "He wants me dead."

"The head of the Consortium?"

"That's what I figure."

"How did you come by this? He commissioned your services, Rath." She rolled her eyes. "I don't deny that what he spoke was woodness, but I don't know if I'd call him sinister."

"The Boreas, the Zephyr, he was using me and then sizing me up. That old man is under his thumb. He wouldn't tell me to whom his horses go, but horses that nice aren't raised for modest traders and travellers; they're raised for noble courts. . . and such courts are benefitted by magicians. They know each other; I'm certain of it."

"You think Orien is responsible for the Zephyr, too? How can you be so sure of this?"

"Orien obviously wanted that Boreas dead so that the people of Gundrada would think him capable of such a deed; let's not forget his deranged maundering about contemporary magic. Notice, also, how we didn't get the credit for slaying the beast." He elongated his words, slightly vexed. "And Zephyrs don't hunt the lands of Bero, Sela. He's testing my strength for some reason. Our line of work is about to get hairy."

"I have never doubted your intuition." Gisela bowed her head for a moment in silence, a long moment. To Rathar, it felt like an eternity. "We need to journey to Reliquary," she said at long last.

"Reliquary? That's weeks away, don't tell me you're on about this again," he said flatly.

"It isn't. . . entirely clear, but God has revealed that we must go." Rathar sighed heavily and laid back into the wet leaves that scattered the ground. "All things are revealed there. . . prophecies and fortellings."

"There's no prophecy about me, Sela. I'm a Stalker. I kill aspirmeygs to save arses that can't wipe themselves. Just so we can live. It's a simple life we lead, and you contrive to complicate it with your religious nonsense."

"You know. . ." Gisela's voice went quiet, "that you're different. You're not like the others, not one bit. You don't even need me."

Rathar sat up quickly and grabbed Gisela by both arms. "Don't say that." His eyes pierced hers, and she felt embarrassed.

"So what do you suggest we do," he said after a while, "until we get to Reliquary? Play dumb? Take Orien's jobs and play along?"

"What else can we do?" Gisela ran her hand over the sore, raised marks along Rathar's chest where the Zephyr had gnashed its massive teeth. Stalkers had superior healing abilities, but it would leave a mark. "We have to be careful, and you need to let me help you shift back to conserve your energy. We don't know what kind of danger could be afoot anymore." She stood and dusted off her long, dark Vestal's robes. "But first, a new shirt for you. I seriously can't mend that." She smiled and held her hand outstretched. Rathar took it firmly, but instead of standing, he pulled her swiftly into the wet, speckled leaves with a laugh. "I can't keep up with your moods!" Gisela huffed, untangling leaves from her golden hair. He wondered to himself how long he would enjoy laughter; what was Orien's plan? Would Reliquary actually reveal anything? But he said none of these things out loud.

Chapter

03

"UGH." RATHAR CLENCHED ONE HAND to his aching stomach. "I'm sick of keeping off the road. We need a Temple. We need money. We need food."

"We have—"

"If you offer me another cursed apple, I'm going to chew it up and spit it at you." Rathar closed his eyes, deeply inhaling through his nose. "What I would give for blood sausages and garlic fried in oil with some crusty bread." Rathar's stomach audibly growled. "I'm going to hunt something; I'll settle for a catch."

"Let me." Gisela stood and stretched her arms over her head.

"I'd be faster." Rathar smirked.

"I think it's best we avoid shifting if we can. It takes energy."

"I don't know what you're so worried about. We're in the middle of the woods."

"That Orien catches us off guard when you're tired or weakened. Anyway, do you doubt my ability to trail? I was crafted by your very hands."

"Leave worrying about Orien to me, Sela. I'm hale, and I'm hungry. Hurry back."

Gisela tiptoed into the woods. She had not the perceptions of a Stalker to guide her, but she had mother wit about her, and when it came to *stalking* she had been reared by the best, in her mind after all, and according to her wits she had heard the howl of a were-dog to the north on their traipse through the woods, which is why Rathar had veered slightly south. Gisela retraced her steps a bit and then headed north. She scrutinized the foliage for a bent branch, a footprint, anything that would tell her she was on the right path, until finally she found a few stray silvery hairs caught in the bramble and reflecting in the moonlight. Were-dogs' hairs had argent tips. "It seems I was right." She moved more swiftly this time, still scanning the backdrop of the forest for clues, but tracks were difficult to follow in the soft berth of deeply bedded needles. *What would Rathar do?* Gisela thought. *He would say, you silly citternhead, you should have let me go if you were going to let it run off; now I shall be hungry and complain all the night for it.* Gisela shook her head. *No the oils on the fur were still fresh; they had lustre. It is not too far off. Now, what would the braggart do?* Gisela cupped her hands around her mouth and made a melancholy howl that rang through the forest. She waited a moment and repeated the howl once more. *Come on now.* She waited a moment in anticipation. *My impressions of Rathar may be shit, but that were-dog was impressive if I do say so myself.* Suddenly a howl circled back through the trees. It was closer than she had imagined. Gisela howled once more, drawing the were-dog nearer. She crept through the thicket, following its cries until she could see it. A were-dog was a skittish, but also a curious creature. Though it was following the sound of her mock bays, she would have to take it by surprise. Gisela crouched behind the shrub that concealed her, but the were-dog caught her scent. It lifted its nose into the air to smell out any presence of danger, and Gisela took the chance to act. She lunged out of the shrub with her dagger drawn and her aim was true; the blade punctured the beast's esophagus and with a tearing motion she severed half the neck cleanly. The were-dog fell to the needles, bleeding profusely. Gisela stabbed it in the heart to kill it once and for all, for its wounds were only temporary. She had learned from Rathar that the only way to kill a were-beast was to stop its heart or else all other injuries would mend as if due to some sort of restorative magic. He said they would even grow new heads if severed, a thought that gave her a sour stomach when she thought of it too much. Then Gisela took a fair bit of rope and tied the limbs of the were-dog, and then hoisted the rope over her shoulder, dragging it back to camp.

•• ———— ••●•• ———— ••

"Were-dog. Delicious." Rathar sat up onto his elbows as Gisela dragged her catch into camp. "Did you. . ."

"Pierce its heart? I'm no fool."

"Indeed." Rathar was beaming. He always looked that way when Gisela slaughtered something or wielded her blade by and large.

"Well, help me with it. I did the hard work. You can at least get your hands a bit dirty." Gisela began unfastening the ropes and Rathar plucked the dagger from his boot.

* * *

Gisela opened her eyes and yawned so widely that her eyes watered, and the tears of forenoon rolled down her cheek. What patches of the sky could be seen were painted over with pink and lavender as the sun had barely risen. Rathar had wrapped up the remaining meat from the night and was adjusting his load. "Let's go," he rasped and held out Gisela's pack.

"Let me wash my face in the stream just that way." Gisela placed the pack on the ground, carrying nothing but her bronze blade at her side. She walked leisurely through the wood toward the stream, its babbling as her guide. She admired its crystalline clarity, almost as clear as the glassy water that cascaded down from the ashlar fountain in the grassy courtyard at the Abbey back home. She knelt down onto her outer garment which she had folded beside the bank and scooped the water up toward her face. A second scoop, gazing through its lucid rush at the polished stones beneath. A third, but this time she stopped, the water a mirror in her hands. Behind her was a face gazing into her little pool, beautiful yet sinister. The water fell from her hands as she drew her blade and it rang out with an echo and a clang as it met a scaly arm, hard as iron. The creature hissed and bared a mouth full of terrible, pearlescent fangs. Gisela's sword was swift, but the creature had speed to match; each swing of the blade was blocked by armoured scales, magnificent blues and greens glinting in the sunlight now starting to peek through the trees. Blow for blow neither could outwit the other, the creature lunging with her vicious bite and Gisela deflecting with her long blade. Finally, in one swift movement the creature's strong, plated arm pressed Gisela against the rough bark of a tree, rendering her unable to break free or swing her sword. Before the creature could dive in to feast, Gisela saw four bronze gimlet spikes burst through the abdomen of her adversary and watched it go limp to reveal Rathar standing behind, holding the creature by her knotted, blue hair. Gisela's shoulders dropped in relief.

"A river-shrew." Rathar dragged the creature by her hair back to the stream and tossed its lifeless body in, the clear water running crimson. "It was tethered to this stream." He turned back and picked up Gisela's blade from the ground, wiping the damp leaves onto his trouser leg. "Not bad." He handed the sword back to Gisela who was examining the blood spattered on her robes. "You almost had it." Rathar smiled, concealing his true sentiment which was that of concern. She should have had it. Gisela had been trained by his very hands; a creature so common as a river-shrew should have been simple work at her hands. "We'll make a Stalker of you yet," he added lightly, noting the dark rings of purple below her eyes. The two continued on through the thick of woods headed south toward Lanthchilde. They meant to avoid the western mountain pass of Rotrude, for winter was on their heels. They would take the vast Adonican Plains which skirted the mountain range, and then north to Reliquary via the connecting Scaenus Plains and edging forests. Rathar spoke after what seemed like leagues of silence. "We will make quick work of Lanthchilde."

"They are friendly to Stalkers there, that's what the stableman said, and we've always known it to be a truth." While Gisela spoke, she rubbed the irksome, burning spot on her neck. Rathar squinted back at Gisela in concern.

"I just have a feeling. . . we shouldn't stay long. I say we stock up, we rest outside the city, and we leave." Rathar wasn't keen on being too long in a place at the behest of anyone he suspected to be in league with Orien.

"You could use a bath." Gisela laughed weakly. "And I'll need to buy you a new tunic and jerkin at least."

"A waste of silver when rivers and rags suit me adequately," Rathar grumbled. Gisela only rolled her eyes.

"You've not been sleeping. That's why you're so grouchy." She hooked her arm through his, but Rathar noticed a weight in her step. "We'll stay at the Temple tonight, flinders for a bed instead of stones." Rathar said nothing, his usual method of admitting defeat, and Gisela grinned, pleased with herself. They reached Lanthchilde by midafternoon, a bit slower than Rathar would have liked, but Gisela was not as swift as she usually was; he chalked it up to her struggle that morning. Lanthchilde was a bright and bustling city built into the side of a massive, marble deposit; everything glistened and gleamed in splendid white. "It's a good thing your cloak is dark; I could lose you here where you look the same as the stone." Gisela looked in awe around her, reaching out her fingers to touch the chilly carvings of hewn-out buildings and etchings as they passed. "Many times I have been to Lanthchilde, but each time the beauty is new to me." They walked through the streets attracting the unusually sullen points and stares of children playing with wooden swords, one who tried to lance Rathar in the rear; maids selling their wares whispered snobbishly, and men pulling carts went out of their way to put distance between them until they reached an inn carved out of the same glistening white stone where a red-faced man with bulbous cheeks grinning widely caught Rathar by the elbow.

"Stalker, eh?" the red-faced man said. "Lucky you came my way, master Stalker! I'll take care of ye." The man grinned even bigger if it were possible. "I be the innkeeper here." He patted his belly and took out his purse. Rathar's attention was elsewhere as he noticed the beads of sweat on Gisela's brow despite the chilly autumn air.

"I'm afraid we've no business at the inn today sir. We'll be staying at the Temple," Gisela replied politely.

"I'm afraid not, Miss!" The Temple is on the west side of town, and you'd better stay on the east side of town if you know what's good for ye, bein' a Vestal an' all. I'm afraid ye won't be reachin' the Temple from here."

"Is Lanthchilde not known to be hospitable to Stalkers and Vestals?" Gisela mused.

"Oh sure, always in the old times. But now ye see, we have a bit of an uprisin' on our hands. The west side is all blockaded. They ain't allowin' no Stalkers through ye see. No Vestals neither."

"Whatever for?"

"They're holdin' them captive. Got themselves a Stalker who massacred some burgages on the east side of town, the Vestal too who stood by and did nothing. They say they're gonna bring 'em to justice publicly. Ye know. . . kill 'em." The innkeeper slid his fingers across his throat and widened his eyes. "Now they ain't friendly to no Stalkers and no Vestals. The city is split ye see." Gisela turned toward Rathar who was all ears now, brow furrowed and hanging on every word.

"Why would a Stalker massacre homes in town?" Rathar pressed. "The bloodlust does not arise unless he starts killing; you're telling me he either killed a beast in the streets of Lanthchilde, which is highly unlikely, or that he was killing *a person*."

"He could have killed a rabid dog for alls I know, master Stalker, and don't tell me that you lot are above killing men. A sword's a sword; it slits the throat of the one that offends it." The innkeeper shrugged. Rathar still thought it peculiar that a trained Vestal, nay a woman of God, seeing the bloodlust rise in her Stalker, would stand aside and watch a massacre of innocent lives take place.

"Do you know who. . ." Gisela started, "who. . ." her words slurred and everything around her began to spin. The warm light of the sun faded into a bleary glow before dying out beneath closed eyes. Rathar was astonished as he held her, inches from the ground where she had nearly fallen. As he held her there, the neck of her robes had slipped back to reveal what looked like a scar, only it was in a perfect circle with a delicate filigree inside – a magician's seal – a curse mark.

"Oh dear!" The red-faced man never stopped grinning, "happy to accommodate you, right this way; we'll get the young lady a bed, and I can summon the magician to cure what ails ye."

"Bring me no magician." Rathar scowled and scooped Gisela up effortlessly, following the innkeeper through a maze of carved hallways. They entered a room of modest size and Rathar laid Gisela onto the bed. "Where is the apothecary?" He turned toward the innkeeper, who was still grinning like a fool; it was starting to get on Rathar's nerves.

"I'm afraid ye won't be goin' there. Wrong side of the city ye see. No place for Stalkers. Not with this uprisin'."

"I'm going," he snarled.

"They'll never let ye in, young master, or out!" The innkeeper laughed. Rathar pulled the mighty, gleaming long-sword of bronze from his side and hoisted it with one strong arm over his shoulder.

"I think they'll find me convincing. Look after her. *No magicians*," he impressed and left the innkeeper who had stopped grinning.

•• ——— ••●•• ——— ••

Rathar made his way to the east side of the city cloaked and hooded. Gisela had been cursed with a magician's mark, and time was against him in destroying it, so his endeavour was to be as inconspicuous as possible. The line between east and west in the city was morose. Fires burned here and there with rowdy shouts, people guarded the boundary with arms, shouting slurs as those on the west passed by. There was no way by which Rathar could enter without being seen. He approached the border with his face down.

"I need to reach the apothecary."

"Why?" A man of medium stature, armed with only a short sword, cocked his head in defiance.

"That's my business."

"You want to pass this border? *Your* business is *my* business." Rathar looked up with eyes full of poison. "Backwater bastard," the man chortled under his breath. "You don't belong here, Stalker. It's your lucky day, I'm letting you walk free, now leave." He spat on Rathar's boots. Rathar's gaze was steady and icy as death.

"The apothecary." He said again trying to control his temper, patience wearing thin.

"I don't think you heard me, Stalker. Don't you have a Vestal to make you behave?"

"She's sick. I need the apothecary," he said, letting out a growl from deep in his belly.

"Plenty of those walking around, pick you out a new one at Reliquary can't ya? Leave this one for the wolves in Terrowin."

"She is neither horse nor dog."

"I'll tell you what she is, Stalker. She's a puppet master." The man began to chuckle but not for long as Rathar had him pinned against the ground in seconds with blade gently tracing a line painfully across his whiskered Adam's apple. Inconspicuousness be damned.

"The apothecary."

"D. . . down th. . . that road. I. . . I don't want any t. . . trouble. Honest," the man sniveled.

"Spineless coward." Rathar pressed his dusty boot into the man's cheek before making his way down the road and toward the apothecary. It could only have been described as a shanty, held up by a prayer and poorly put together planks, but with a juxtaposing, beautifully carved sign sporting a fleur-de-lis that read *Lily of the Valley Apothecary*. The inside was just as lacklustre; a dim-lit, little cave of a place, stuffed full of overcrowded shelves from floor to ceiling. Some holding vials of different coloured liquids, some holding jars of curious objects from fresh and dried roots and leaves to the severed parts of both familiar and unfamiliar animals. There was a bug-eyed fellow with enormous, round glasses carefully tweezing purple spines from a long, green stalk resting in a short vase of murky water behind a counter when Rathar entered. The bug-eyed fellow was absorbed in the task and hadn't even seen him, so Rathar coughed a little to make his presence known.

"Oh, oh yes, my, my," he chattered very quickly. "Why I haven't had a customer here since the blockade. The name is Wells, what can I do for you dear sir, yes, yes what can I do?"

"I need a measure of milk thistle, a measure of mugwort, a measure of adderwort, and a quarter of a measure of distilled henbane oil. Quickly as you can." Rathar tossed a leather purse onto the counter filled with silver coins and shifted his position to show his impatience. He inhaled the herbaceous, vinegary smells of the apothecary almost greedily. He'd always had a knack for herbs, and he loved the complexity, yes, the challenge a root or a petal could present with its many constituents all working in harmony to heal an affliction or many afflictions.

"Yes, yes, right away, dear sir. But that is a nasty concoction you have there, for a magical seal, am I right?" Rathar did not answer, but only crossed his arms over his chest to signify that he was waiting. The bug-eyed man flitted about the shelves, moving this out of the way, knocking this over, pouring a bit of something into an empty vial, and tweezing shreds of something else into another. Finally, he wrapped up the package neatly in a sack of what Rathar smelled to be goat skin and tied it up, presenting it to Rathar, and taking the little leather purse for himself. "Good luck to you, dear sir, yes. Good luck I say. Take a bit of this burdock for the, the scar. Yes, free of charge."

"Thanks for the hospitality, Wells."

The man pushed his glasses up his nose with a goofy but kind-hearted smile. Rathar made his way back over the barricade, giving a good kick in the arse to the guard for good measure who curled up in on himself when he saw Rathar approaching, and found himself back at the inn in no time at Gisela's bedside mixing his potion. The final mixture was like a paste which he tried gingerly, which was still roughly for him, to slather over the curse mark on Gisela's neck. He then tied a bandage around it so that her robes would not rub the precious mixture off. Milk thistle had anti-magical and curse breaking properties; it should be able to lift the curse in time. The only hang up was that it was ghastly expensive if you didn't know where to get it yourself, and Rathar was nowhere near a natural supply all the way out in Lanthchilde which suddenly felt very much like a stony prison. He'd spent every silver piece. All he could do now was wait, and wait he did, hardly leaving Gisela's side. The innkeeper often brought food in to him, for he could not be torn from the room over his anxiety and watchkeeping. He watched her breath, making sure that her chest continued to fall gently up and down. He watched her face, making sure that the colour never drained suddenly. He watched her fingers twitch and dance in her prolonged sleep, making sure that her body never went still. He felt her skin, assuring that it was still warm and not chilly and stiff. He watched her for four days before her eyelids, cracking open, met his, then drooped shut again in a mild doze.

"Rath?" She mumbled. He sighed hugely, dramatically, relieved and threw his head back against the stone wall.

"Let me see." He pulled her close by the shoulders and examined her neck. The seal was gone. All that remained was a white, scarred blur of skin, though less pronounced thanks to Wells's complimentary herbs.

"Rathar. . . what happened?"

"Don't worry about that now. How do you feel?" he asked, trying to conceal a yawn.

"How long have I been sleeping?" She winced at a bed sore on her back.

"Four days."

"Four days!" she gasped.

"You were cursed. It wasn't your fault. But you're alright now."

"Rathar, I must know what happened."

"Not now, Sela." He pushed her shoulder back into the pillow. "Rest."

"Sit beside me." She could see his bloodshot eyes were weary. "You lost sleep over me all this time." He sat on the edge of the too small bed. "I'll rest if you do."

"Sela. . ." But he was interrupted by her warm hand on the back of his neck, a familiar trick that he could not escape. He felt his eyes close, and his body fall, curled up on the side of the bed next to her warm body. It was not a sleep he could fight against, and within seconds he succumbed to the dark behind his lids. Gisela leaned back against the pillow, still sitting upright. She was tired, too, still not entirely recovered from the curse. She closed her eyes and soon dozed off to the sound of Rathar's gentle snoring beside her.

•• ———— ••●•• ———— ••

It was evening when Gisela opened her eyes again. Rathar had already woke before her and was content to sit at the end of the bed, leaning against the tall post of the frame, sharpening his boot knife with a piece of porous stone. "That's a devilish trick of yours," he said, not looking up from his task.

"You feel better now, though, don't you?" He did not reply, but only continued to scrape the stone against the side of the short blade rhythmically.

"Sela."

"Yes?"

"How do you feel?"

"Refreshed, really. But rather sore and stiff from lying here for so long."

"Good, that's good." There were a few moments of silence before Rathar continued, "Then I have a few questions for you."

"Go on."

"You were cursed. . ."

"Yes, by the old man in Bero."

Rathar looked up, astonished. "By the old man in Bero," he repeated, but slowly as if every word were heavy on his tongue.

"Yes, he touched my neck here." She reached for the smooth scar. "And it burned like fire, but I didn't think a moment about it because in you came with the head of a Zephyr at just the same time."

Rathar's face was serious and stony. "A ceded curse. Tricky to perform. They originate from a magician but are handed off to another for administration. A thousand things can go wrong. Tell me, did it trouble you soon after?"

"Only a bit, but I must confess, I really didn't think much of it. I'd forgotten about the old man and just thought the burning sensation a nuisance. That is, until I started to feel so ill."

"I admit." He pursed his lips, "I thought something was wrong from the moment that river-shrew almost overtook you." Gisela cast her eyes down, embarrassed. "Well, I think this is only further proof. Orien and the man from Bero are conspiring." Rathar set aside the porous stone and the dagger and dragged his palms across his face in exasperation. "We can trust no one."

"Rath." Gisela stuck her tongue in her cheek as she often did when she was in thought; Rathar had always thought it a peculiar mannerism of hers. "Why would Orien have me cursed? What does it matter if I am dead or alive?" her words echoed in her head, her own impotence like another curse that had not been healed. "They suspect that you're beyond my influence and have been for a long time. So, tell me, why does it matter?"

"It matters a great deal." Rathar suddenly stood up and began to pace the room. "Perhaps Orien didn't think that we'd catch on to this ruse, but I think he was taking precautions. I think he discerned that if we *did catch on*, we'd make straight for Reliquary, so just in case. . ." Rathar lowered his voice almost to a whisper.

"Just in case, he thought it'd be best to do away with me, the only Vestal who can read your prophecies at Reliquary," Gisela whispered back. "For some reason, Orien thinks you have a prophecy in Reliquary. . . a prophecy worth something."

Rathar ignored her last statement deliberately. "Sela, we can't have this warlock predicting our moves. We can't go straight to Reliquary; it'd be walking into a trap we set for ourselves. The road is likely perilous until he is sure. . . you're dead." Rathar pinched his nose between his fingers pensively, "No, we must delay somewhere, somewhere safe."

"Borghild," they both said at once.

"Yes. That is the safest place I know. Borghild," Rathar confirmed.

"It is impossible to find unless you know the way," Gisela agreed. Rathar cursed under his breath. "What is it?"

"We'll require horses if we are to make it there before winter becomes cruel, but we can't reach the Temple here, and I spent every coin we had. . ."

"On what?" Gisela sucked in her breath, but then caught sight of the little porcelain jars sitting on the bedside table that smelled of strong medicine. Rathar saw her scrutiny and cast his eyes down.

Gisela fidgeted for a moment with her robes before noticing that the one she wore most outwardly was draped over a chair by the window, still decorated with the river-shrew's blood. "Reach in the left pocket over there, Rathar. Reach in and find the little bag of green velvet."

"This one?"

"Yes, open it up."

He dumped the contents of the small bag onto his open palm and was astonished to see four shining, moderately sized rubies. "Where did you get these!?"

"Take them and buy horses, some proper tack, and whatever else we need to get to Borghild and respite the winter there." Gisela was beginning to lose her breath, and she could feel herself sinking back into the goose down pillow. "Stop staring at me and do as I say. Leave me to rest and go do these errands."

Rathar's mouth was still agape. "Is this your Vestal's dowry?"

"I have saved it for a need as dire as this." Gisela spoke almost in a whisper now; she could feel what little energy she had draining from her body. "Rath, go."

He nodded and did not argue further but turned on his heel clutching the treasure in his fist.

04

DEAD BRANCHES AND BRAMBLE CRACKED and crunched under hooves as Rathar and Gisela tramped onward through the woods of Rowan, now west toward the mountain pass of Rotrude. It was a way they knew well; Rathar admired the woods of Rowan. They were some of the first wilds he trekked as a fresh Stalker thrust out from the bosom of Borghild charged with the duty of protecting the Provinces. He preferred a forest to most anywhere, especially the displeasing congestion of a city, and Rowan, as far as forests went, was a splendid one with towering, pines and fragrant cedars. The paths were covered with a thick cushion of pine needles and treefall that felt supple underfoot, a welcome reprieve to the trudge of hard trails and rough roads that was tiresome to the treads of boots. Rathar held at his side the reins of a small pack pony laden with supplies, the first time they'd been laden with *anything* in a long while. Rathar looked frequently behind at his companion, wrapped in cloaks and slumped over in her saddle; though the seal had been eradicated, Gisela still wasn't well, but they'd had no choice but to journey on. To stay in one place too long was now wholly unsafe. They had to make for the keep of Borghild as soon as possible to wait out at least the beating heart of winter and try to elude their newfound enemies. The sun was disappearing slowly as dusk settled on the woods, and Rathar halted their ride for the first time since morning. He lifted Gisela's drooping figure off of the horse she had affectionately named Lief and propped her up against a tree as he made a comfortable little camp for the night. The darkness brought with it a chill as winter approached, and Gisela had wrapped around her three scratchy, wool cloaks as well as hovering around the small fire Rathar had built. "Drink this." Rathar held a canteen to Gisela's lips so that she would not have to unwrap her arms from their wooly cocoon; he had mixed what was left of the henbane with the water to help Gisela with what remained of her illness. She sipped and then slumped back against the tree. "Sleep if you can," Rathar rasped, "I'm afraid that tomorrow will be much like today; we don't have much time to waste. We have to keep riding."

"Tell me," Gisela smiled, "about Borghild. About being a boy."

"You don't usually ask about this sort of thing. The upbringing of Stalkers so pricks your tender heart." Rathar wasn't lying. Much of his childhood at Borghild was a blur of cold nights, hard days, feelings. . . harshness, strain, sometimes fear, though all blended with a strange concoction of love. Gisela had struggled in the past to understand rearing children in such an environment.

"Did you ever pick flowers?"

"No," Rathar laughed out loud.

"I picked lovely flowers at Reliquary," Gisela sighed, "for my mistress. It pleased her very much to see what little things I could find. Lilies, daisies, sometimes a wild rose or a bunch of snowdrops. She would smile at me like a mother in love with her daughter."

"Do you remember your real mother?" Rathar said quietly.

"I do not. She couldn't afford to feed me; I know that, so she left me with the sisters at Reliquary when I was just a little thing." More silence. Sometimes Rathar felt that Gisela heard words unspoken in his silence, warm words that his gruffness did not make it easy to express. Perhaps it was one of her Vestal's gifts, perhaps a distaff trait, or perhaps, yet more likely, it was the years of friendship that had bonded them after all this time. "Rath. . . do you remember your mother?"

Gisela watched the light of the flames dance on Rathar's pale face. It was stony, undeviating, and gave nothing away.

"Rath. . ."

"Yes?"

"Nothing." Gisela looked down and pulled the cloaks tighter around her. "That potion has given me some strength."

"Reserve it. And sleep." Rathar poked the fire with a stick and after a while of watching the sparks gently float up into the air, the wood around her darkened behind tired lids, and Gisela slept.

•• ———— ••●•• ———— ••

Gisela awoke to the smell of something sweet. She inhaled deeply, eyes still closed. What was it, a plant of some kind? A small bunch of winter heather tied with a white ribbon. She sat up quickly, and the little bouquet which had been placed on her chest fell to her lap.

"Does it please you? To see what I can find?" Rathar smiled.

"Where did you find such a treasure?" Gisela's voice was a song in the stillness of the wood in the morning. "I am pleased indeed!" She stood, standing taller than yesterday.

"The colour has come back to your cheeks," Rathar said, relieved. He took the little bouquet resting in her cupped hands, as gingerly as he could, and tucked it into Lief's bridle. "You know. . . giving someone winter heather means you believe in their ability to overcome difficult situations."

"It also symbolises sorrow," Gisela whispered to herself.

"What was that?"

"Won't your horse be jealous to walk next to such a pretty thing?" Gisela grinned wide, patting Lief's neck affectionately as Rathar lifted her into the saddle and climbed into his own saddle, grabbing the reins of the pack pony. "If you must give me that awful tasting draught, then do, for we can't have you wandering about without your mother, can we?" Gisela beamed, touching the petals of the little bouquet. "Oh how pleased I am."

My mother, indeed. Rathar thought. *She tells me when she's pleased with me. She all but thrashes me when she's angry. She buys me new clothes, and tells me when to bathe. She makes me sleep when I'm weary, even when I'd rather stay up. Yes, I'm pleased to pick flowers for my little mother.* He smiled.

"What is it? Have you thought of a name for your horse?"

"No," Rathar grunted, "No, it isn't that."

"What about Rolf?"

"No."

"Dain then."

"I'm not naming the damned horse."

"You're not fun at all." *A mother and a child all in one.* Rathar chuckled. "Oh come now, you're smiling and laughing and not sharing the joke."

"I'm just happy to see such life in you today. That henbane worked well."

"Yes." Gisela bit her lip. "It did, didn't it?" They trekked on much in the same way as they had been, only faster than before, through the woods hoping to break through them onto a short plain that would take them to the mountain pass of Rotrude. Gisela was tired of the woods, tired of the canopy that reached over and around them like an unwelcome embrace. Rathar, on the other hand, didn't mind the cover of trees; it offered concealment and protection from prying eyes and unfortunate company. They walked on and on, watching the hot breath of the horses puff clouds into the chill air, crunching and cracking through the forest floor until about midafternoon.

"Rathar, look!" Gisela pulled back gently on Lief's reins and rested her hands on the horn of her saddle. "The edge of Rowan." The edge of the forest crept before them and revealed a wide plain of tall, wild grass lying flat on account of the vicious wind that had previously been obstructed by the thick forest, and throughout the grasses were sprinkled boulders and slabs of stones of varying sizes. Now all that lay between the wood and the mountain pass was a flatland decimated by a frigid gale. Lief tossed his head and stomped his feet in protest as his ears twitched at the eerie whistle. "Don't worry, Lief." Gisela watched as the wind caught the little bouquet of heather and dragged it across the plain in a flurry of petals. She reached for them in vain.

"The wind cannot deter us. We have to make it to the pass tonight; there's nowhere to camp otherwise," Rathar instructed, obviously as excited about the change in weather as Lief was. Gisela reached over and pulled Rathar's woolen hood over his ears, securing it tightly with a leather cord. She then did the same with her own cloak, and kicked her heels gently into Lief's sides, encouraging him to step out onto the blustery plain.

•• —————— ••●•• —————— ••

They were middling the plain when the first, wisping boulder crashed and crumbled to pieces, narrowly missing the left flank of Lief. He reared in fear, nearly knocking Gisela off into the tall grass.

"What was that?" Gisela shrieked, trying to get her wits about her, but finding herself disoriented as the wind whipped her golden curls across her face and eyes. Rathar immediately stopped his horse and luckily, too, as another boulder came flying through the air only to land right in front of him. His horse reared, and he landed hard on his backside. Quickly he grabbed the reins of his horse and pack pony and shoved them toward Gisela who had hopped off of Lief and tied her hair back with a piece of ribbon.

"Find the best cover you can." He waved his hand generally toward a sprinkling of large rocks. "A Boreas dwells here!" He had to shout to be heard above the howling. Gisela did not hesitate, and with a little difficulty, pulled the three horses, against the wind, toward some shelter. Rathar looked toward the sky, another pale, cloudlike boulder conjured up by the Boreas was closing in on where he stood. Quickly he drew his bronze sword, no ordinary sword by the standards of men, but one enhanced by magic; he held it out like a bat for a game, and his arms and hands were just barely splotched with dull shades of ruby. As the boulder reached its target he swung at it, following through with strong arms, and the boulder disintegrated into a pile of remnants around him. Rathar noted the source of the boulder and ran toward it, wrestling against the wind. The beast stood two men tall, with massive limbs and glowing, yellow eyes, dragging its hideous whetted claws along the ground.

"Can't sleep with this gusting? I don't blame you." Rathar smirked and turned his sword on the creature. Ruddy blotches on his hands and arms traveled up his neck and around his face, his eyes just slightly growing over with muted tissue. "You stink." He grimaced, and lunged at the creature, aiming for the knees. The Boreas was impressively fast for its lumbering size, and jumped away, dodging the move, but Rathar turned as the Boreas stepped sideways and slashed behind one of its monstrous hinges. Now the Boreas was limping, and angry. With its good leg, it kicked Rathar hard, sending him flying into the slab of real rock behind him. Rathar crawled back onto his feet, adrenaline carrying his weight. He set his focus on the other leg of the beast, shaking off the double vision that had come from hitting his head on the rock slab. The Boreas reached down for a wisping boulder materializing before it, aiming to throw it toward Gisela and the horses; but Rathar approached it from behind, almost nonchalantly, and heaved with his sword above his shoulders, crippling the beast as it collapsed before him, and the boulder which it meant to hurl across the gusty plain came toppling down onto its shuddering belly. Once more, Rathar swung his sword with all his might, looking into its ugly, glowing yellow eyes with purpose and watched the great head lop off into a purple pool, his favourite method. The wind blew tendrilled remains of the Boreas hither and thither as Rathar resheathed his sabre and made his way back to Gisela and the horses, head still slightly spinning. Upon reaching her, Gisela was surprised to see Rathar's shining hazel eyes framed by patches of vermilion.

"Rath," she almost had to shout though they were very close. "You shifted incompletely!" He said nothing but only took the reins of his horse and the pack pony and leapt into the saddle, arms and hands still faintly flickering red. He nodded his head west, and Gisela mounted her own horse and followed him across the remainder of the blustery plain to the mountain pass, understanding that it was both impractical and irritating to try and communicate while they were stuck in the clutches of the gales.

•• ——— ••●•• ——— ••

Once they arrived at a shelter of trees, the path began to ascend. "Here we are," Rathar said nonchalantly. The bruises had nearly left him, and he was returning to his characteristic ashen colour. "The mountain pass of Rotrude. It looks as if we've made it just in time." He held out his hand and several tiny snowflakes fell gently and melted on his palm. Gisela tossed her head back, vexed, and looked away. Rathar raised an eyebrow and smirked. "Since you're acting like a spoilt princess, I'll respond in kind, 'Yes, your highness?'" Gisela felt her face turn red up to the tops of her ears and her blood boiled within her. She threw down the reins of her horse and hopped off the saddle, approaching Rathar with stomping and white-knuckled fists; she didn't know why or what would come of it.

"Don't you know you could have been killed by that Boreas?" she was shouting. She was aware of it in a vague way, but she couldn't very well stop herself. "You didn't even shift! You just damn well went after it! It threw you against that rock, but it could have done much worse, you know! I know you're strong and brave, but you can't just fight aspirmeygs like that! Maybe you can handle a river-shrew, or an elf, or a dwarf, or a man, but not an aspirmeyg. That's not how it's done!"

I'd say this was rather funny if she weren't so upset. Rathar hid a chuckle deep within himself. "Sela. . ."

"And I'm not a spoilt princess. I'm angry!"

"I can see that." Rathar remained composed which only made Gisela feel worse about herself in the present moment. "Sela, I had no time to shift; that Boreas and its stones came out of nowhere. Do you understand?" Gisela twisted her foot in the grass uprooting the blades and leaving a spot of mud where her boot was. He was lying. She knew it. He could shift in an instant, had shifted in an instant.

"Your burdens are heavy. You're distracted," she murmured.

"Gisela."

"Don't lie to me, Rathar." Her grey eyes glistened. "We have known each other too long for that."

"I chose not to shift," he sighed; her eyes could break him. "Yes, I was. . . distracted." Gisela looked down at her feet again. Rathar reached down and lifted her chin. "No sullen faces now. Look around you. Open your mouth, wide like this, and catch the flakes on your tongue." Rathar stuck his tongue out under the falling snowflakes like he used to do as a boy. "Come now, show me a smile. I do dislike to see you upset." Gisela smiled a bit and remounted her horse. "Let's get going now. Once we make it over the pass, we'll navigate the tricks of the swamp. Nothing like cold bog water in your boots to cheer you up."

Chapter

05

THE SLATE-GREY, STONY FACADE OF Borghild loomed out of the mist that hung over the swamp that concealed itself behind the mountain pass of Rotrude. The wet cold clung desperately to the trees with low-hanging, sloppy branches and mud that could swallow a man or a beast. The swamp gurgled and breathed hideously, and if one did not know the way, it was certainly a perilous path to tread. The walls of the keep were tall and weathered but had remained impenetrable for all their years and loomed above the curtain like a beacon. Borghild had served as the Stalkers' home for generations; it was well hidden in the damp of the morass, not far from the land of their native race, the wights, so called because the races of the Provinces so rarely saw them that they believed them to be as spectres dwelling as ghosts in the mountains, and because the nobler designation of Stalker had been unceremoniously torn from them long ago after a feud with magicians of old. One could not find Borghild unless he knew exactly the way, and it was well guarded with various natural traps leading up to its sturdy, high walls. It was also protected by another force, a force that juxtaposed the ugliness of the swamp with an elegant power. Rathar and Gisela crossed the drawbridge and approached the massive oak doors trimmed with iron straps and buckles, and carved ornately with the lofty leaning willow trees and other flora indigenous to the area. Rathar reached into his saddlebags and pulled out a crimson banner embroidered with a golden scorpion's tail—the insignia of the Stalker; he held it above his head toward the grey turret with a small, dark window. In a few moments, the enormous doors began to swing open, welcoming them into the castle.

"Vivica." Rathar smiled, stuffing the crimson flag back into his bag.

"Rathar, Gisela, it's been too long." Vivica tucked her black hair, which under the sun shone violet, behind her ear; it fell to her waist, exquisite, and matched the dark pigment on her lips and eyes and complimented the shapely, dark blue silk dress that fell just off her shoulders and dusted her black, leather boots. There was also a dainty gold chain around her neck adorned with a golden scorpion's tail.

"I'll take the horses around to the stables. Go ahead and take these supplies inside." Rathar hoisted a few wrapped parcels onto Gisela's shoulders. Once inside Borghild, Vivica broke the gloom with a snap of her fingers, illuminating the warm torches in heavy sconces that lined the hall.

"My darling." Vivica's voice did not sing like Gisela's but rather was smooth and warm like drinking spiced wine. She lifted a few of the packages off of Gisela's shoulders and carried them on her full-figured hip. "It's been lonely these past months." She grinned, tucking her violet locks behind her ear with her free hand. The end of the corridor opened up into a great hall in which there was a large oak table in the middle surrounded by backless, spartan stools. To the left of the table was a monstrous hearth with a roaring, amethyst fire, a colour that Rathar had always thought complemented the mistress's own hair, and he'd always wondered if she'd done it on purpose. *I've missed this magic fire, a flame that won't go out*, Gisela thought, and was grateful on account of the chill outside. To the right of the oak table were various corridors which led to different rooms for sleeping, bathing, and cooking, and to the left were a chancery bursting at the seams with collections and volumes, rooms for storing goods and supplies, a well-stocked armoury, the mistress's private quarters, and in sharp contrast to the rest of the stony enclosure—a courtyard that Gisela knew to be absolutely lavish in the warmer months, which was bedecked with the bare, scraggly branches of plum trees having long lost their blooms under the blanket of snow, for certain a product of magic as none of the various fruits and flowers of Vivica's abundant garden would grow in the soggy marshland of Borghild naturally.

Rathar and Gisela sat on the backless stools, warming themselves around the amethyst flames. Vivica was pouring burgundy wine from a crystal decanter into three matching crystal goblets. "Ladies first." Her dark lips twisted into a soft smile as she passed the crystal goblets around the fire. "Tell me, my darlings, what brings you to Borghild? You've been tight lipped since your arrival, and I may be a magician, but I don't feign to read minds. Especially. . . hardened ones." She raised an eyebrow at Rathar and sipped her wine. "Come then, Sela will tell me. Won't you, dear?" Vivica shifted on her stool turning her body away from Rathar and towards Gisela.

"Vivica, we're weary from our journey. You'll hear nothing tonight." Rathar stood, draining his crystal goblet uncouthly. Vivica had always raised the boys on wine, her personal preference, as opposed to ale, and Rathar still found he had a taste for it every time he returned home despite tavern after tavern of malt to slake him.

"Don't blame me for being curious." Vivica was entirely immune to Rathar's gruffness; she had raised all of the Stalkers who were out and doing their *business* since boyhood, and she knew they were rough around the edges to put it lightly. She pulled a strand of violet hair from across her eye. "I wasn't expecting a single Stalker this winter. Not a one. You boys manage to keep yourselves occupied well enough in these Provinces. Not often do you have a need to return home, unless summoned." She spoke the words slowly and Gisela noticed how prettily the words sat on her lips.

"I'm afraid I'd rather relate our journey to you with Rathar present." Gisela sipped her wine, a little more delicately, fiddling with the scraggly sheepskin rug under her toes.

"Of course, darling." Vivica leaned forward and squinted her eyes. "And then you can tell me all about this pretty thing, I'll be fascinated to hear about it." She ran her cool fingers over Gisela's neck where the indistinct white scar now replaced the old magician's filigree. Nothing was lost on the mistress of Borghild. "It would seem, my friends, that we have left much to be desired this night with words, but do not worry. No ill tidings will find you here." Vivica put her fingers to her lips for a moment as if in thought and then continued, "You will find that I have drawn you baths, and that the rooms are comfortable enough as they have always been. Borghild is safe, so you may sleep in peace, perhaps for the first time in a long time. I won't wake you in the morning; your bodies need rest; the forest floors have been most unkind to you." She tousled Rathar's ruddy hair and ushered them toward the opposite corridors.

Morning came slowly for the guests in Borghild. The sun had already peeked over the foremost mountain encircling the swamp in the distance when Gisela emerged from her room, eyes glassy from sleep. She yawned and watched curiously as Vivica stood in the snow and conjured up beautiful, ripe plums off of the withered, dead branches of the plum trees in the courtyard. Vivica was wearing a floor length dress of golden brocade that fit snugly at the waist, but fell down to the ground in generous pleats, a few of which she had gathered up in her hands to hold the plums which she was harvesting. "Darling, you're awake. Come and help me, won't you?" Vivica's voice broke the silence of the morning that permeated the castle. Gisela stepped out into the courtyard and hunched her shoulders to her ears; it was freezing. "Hold these, please, I'm just going to conjure up a few more for our breakfast." Vivica dumped her collection of plums into Gisela's gathered robes and delicately twisted her fingers round and round the tip of a crooked, grey twig; as she did a green leaf sprouted forth, then it turned into a pretty, pale flower, and then came a ripe, delicious plum which she plucked and put with the rest.

"How can you manage that?" Gisela's voice was a lovely song in the clear quiet of Borghild. "How can you manage to make something alive out of something that's dead?" Vivica smiled and did not answer while she twisted her fingers round the twig again. Gisela watched, enchanted.

"Why, my dear, you have got it all wrong," she finally said, turning toward Gisela and taking half of the plums back into her own pleats. "Magic is the manipulation of potential." She touched the twig gently and caused a green leaf to emerge. "This tree is not dead. If it were, tell me, how would it blossom again come spring? It is simply resting. The potential to bloom and blossom lies latent inside while it rests away the winter; I have merely pulled that potential out of it."

"What about Stalkers?"

"I beg your pardon?"

"Stalkers are killers, but we have manipulated their potential for good; are we magic. . . Vestals I mean? The Abbess always told us that our influence, the power we draw on that can bring a Stalker to do the bidding of even the slightest of clergywomen is from prayer, a power that God provides because he wishes for the goodwill and safety of the Provinces. Do you believe that, Vivica, or would you gamble we're tapped into potential somehow like magicians and petty Diviners?" Gisela had never seriously doubted her faith before, but she had always wondered about the link between magic and prayer. She began placing the plums in an enameled, silver bowl on the great, oak table.

"My darling, Sela, potential lies in and all around us. I can manipulate my words just as much as I can manipulate a man with my charm. Some manipulation, however, such as the manipulation of things that to others seem stationary. . . things like the elements, or even life itself is a magician's gift." Vivica's face was curious.

"I do not have to manipulate Rathar. Even if it was magic, there is none to be found in me."

"Maybe that's the magic in it." Vivica winked. Gisela didn't reply but only looked sorely at the bowl of plums. "Come, darling, eat some breakfast. I insist that you do. You're absolutely gaunt from your travels. What a beating you take on the road, living as no woman should without a proper bath, without any oils and cremes to anoint yourself with, living off of apples and bread, always in the same ragged clothes. I won't permit it here, I simply won't. You're my honoured guest, Gisela. Come, eat up, and we will see what we can do about the dirt under your nails while we wait for that lazy Stalker to wake up; if his pottage gets cold, it's his own fault." Gisela looked down to hide her blushing cheeks, and slowly spooned her pottage into her mouth, not wanting to say that she quite enjoyed the adventuresome beating she took on the road as a simple Vestal.

•• ———— ••●•• ———— ••

Rathar stood, dumbstruck, before the fire in the great hall. She was beautiful, there was nothing else to say. Her crimson dress, a colour he'd never known to be lovely, clung tastefully to a figure he'd never seen before underneath layers of wheaten robes, was adorned with a mink fur belt. Around her shoulders and at the ends of her sleeves sparkled gold, embroidered flowers of a decadent marque. There was nothing on her face, which relieved him, but she smelled of something new. . . plum, and her golden curls bounced around her shoulders, shining like a dragon horde.

"Isn't she lovely?" Vivica tilted Gisela's chin upward with her finger and admired her up and down. "My own work." She smiled and turned toward Rathar. "So, what do you think of your little Vestal? Hmm? She's a Great Lady now. A Duchess! A Princess even! Don't you think she's beautiful?"

"She's always been beautiful," Rathar chuckled, "but I don't think she has ever wanted to be any of those things."

Vivica playfully pouted. "I suppose you're right," she said, twirling Gisela in a circle. "I wonder, though, what potential she has?" She smiled knowingly at Gisela. Rathar squinted in confusion, but Gisela looked down at her feet, embarrassed. "Don't worry, my dear, you can wear your hum-drum robes once they're good and washed. They had so much blood on them; did you know?" Vivica was slightly repulsed. Rathar was tired of talking about clothes.

"Let's talk." He motioned for everyone to sit down on the backless stools.

"What do you know about the magician Orien of Gundrada?" Rathar cracked his knuckles.

"Scheming lunatic," Vivica scoffed.

"And who would take heed of a scheming lunatic in a shitty backwater like Gundrada?; they likely just leave him to his tower," Rathar mused.

"Oh, he has his value, *and his price.* Whatever Orien gets up to in his tower, he purchases with skills," Vivica insisted.

"Gundrada is falling apart. That duchy doesn't look like it's benefitted from a magician in decades," Gisela said.

"Orien is a savage man. I've heard that he works as a hit man for the duke. He gets people out of the way, much quicker than a normal bounty hunter would, and I'm sure in a much nastier way."

"Here I thought the duke was kindly. Feeding the people was the rumour." Rathar furrowed his brow.

"For influence, of course. Power most often attracts power. Orien of Gundrada is head of the Consortium for a reason, darling, because he's *powerful*. Powerful men have ideas, and ideas make enemies... and friends. He has 'novel ideas,' and there's talk he'll even go rogue. Now, there are some rogue magicians here and there, who are not part of the Consortium, but who are friendly towards it... Lily of Cleves and Wellsburg of Lanthchilde to name a few. What these magicians understand is that they live under the laws of the Consortium but not its appropriations; in other words, they're freelancers without resources. Orien of Gundrada is walking a fine line, if you ask me. If he keeps stirring the pot, there might be a pile of ash where he once stood." Vivica covered her pretty lips and chuckled to herself, then turned to Gisela, "No potential, if you know what I mean."

"What do you mean by novel ideas?" Gisela queried.

"Black magic," Vivica purred.

"Don't be a hypocrite now, Viv." Rathar eyed Vivica knowingly.

"Well, it *is* novel. It's been outlawed by the Consortium for centuries! I can think of two magicians who secretly practice it. One was found out and went rogue, and one... well, let's just say, she's not stirring the pot." Vivica smirked.

"He's stirring some pot... though I'm not sure if it's a pot big enough for the Consortium to care about, but you should have heard him prate about Stalkers and magicians." Rathar sighed.

"Vivica, what exactly is black magic?" Gisela asked nervously.

"Well, darling, it's potential like any other magic, but it's destructive and negative potential, coming notably from one's life force such as the blood or one's negative thoughts and intentions, or even the life force of toxic and dangerous plants and herbs."

"So. . . you know black magic?"

"She's a multifaceted woman." Rathar rolled his eyes. "So anyway, back to the pot stirrer."

"Tell me darling." Vivica leaned in and placed her chin on folded hands. "I'm all ears."

Rathar told her about Gundrada, about the Boreas which Orien had captured which she found particularly interesting, and he told her about the old man in Bero and about the Zephyr, and she agreed that there were no Zephyrs in Bero, and then he told her about the river-shrew in the woods, and the filigree curse mark on Gisela's neck during which she nodded intently because she had studied the mark very carefully while Gisela had been bathing, and he told her finally about the Stalker and the Vestal trapped in Lanthchilde which was most displeasing to her, and then Rathar finished his accounts, leaning back on the stool and crossing his arms over his chest to signify his conclusion. Gisela said nothing, only watched both Rathar and Vivica exchange furrowed brows and faces screwed up in thought.

"You were right to seek Borghild," Vivica said after a moment of silence. "No one will find you here, and it would seem bad luck has a habit of seeking you out as of late. But not here, no, not here. Here you are safe." She bit her lip in thought. "It is clear that the Boreas was caught by Orien with purpose, to make Orien look very powerful to the people; and it is clear that the Zephyr was placed, and that the old man in Bero was working for someone. Who, I cannot say unless I see the filigree. It can be guessed that it was Orien, but I cannot say for sure; my God, who has such a power as to *place a Zephyr*? Darling, can you draw it for me? Can you recall the seal?" Rathar nodded. He picked up the fire poker and in the smooth coat of ash on the hearth stone, he drew as he remembered, the filigree that cursed Gisela. Vivica's eyes widened. "Oh, my dear, are you quite sure?" Rathar nodded, silently. "Rathar, that's the filigree of Mirabelle of Dimia."

"Are *you* sure, Viv?" Rathar massaged his jaw with his hand. "Because I think the old man was working for Orien."

"Very sure." She affirmed. "That would be two pot stirrers." She held up two elegant fingers and paused for a moment. "I think this is all a bit larger than you envisioned."

"Reliquary is much too dangerous now, but we definitely must go. Perhaps as soon as spring," Gisela pressed.

"Why does everyone want to take this to Reliquary? It's two 'pot stirrers' that need to be squashed," Rathar growled.

"Everyone who knows you knows that you're. . . different, Rathar." Vivica wasn't smiling. "I can give you information; I can give you support from perhaps part of the Consortium; I can give you asylum. But I can't give you what I think Reliquary can give you. . . I feel it just as strongly as Gisela feels it, all around you, a force of some kind. You'll winter here, but then I insist, you must go seek out your prophecy." Rathar looked at Vivica and Gisela, both were radiant as the sun, bedecked in their gowns, anointed with their oils, both firm and unrelenting in their dispositions, like powerful queens. He put his hands up in surrender, and his queens smiled upon him.

•• ———— ••●•• ———— ••

Winter at Borghild was peaceful. The mornings were restful; Vivica and Gisela would usually prepare breakfast together, and Vivica was especially fond of this on account of having spent so much time alone in the castle or with boys; she especially loved the company of another woman. Gisela and Vivica talked and giggled together while Rathar kept himself always busy and out of the way. In the afternoons, Rathar insisted on physical training so that they wouldn't become lazy and slow; he and Gisela often ran together, sparred, and spent time maintaining their weapons as well as those in the armoury. This was much to the disdain of Vivica who would rather dress up Gisela and parade her around the castle like a princess than watch her sweat and bruise, but after particularly difficult sparring matches, Gisela happily let Vivica run her a soothing, hot bath of chamomile and arnica. On one such evening, Gisela hunched over her knees in the steaming water of the mistress's personal copper soaking tub, rubbing a painful bruise on her shin where Rathar had struck her in a sparring match.

"Darling, it's unfair." Vivica leaned over the tub and touched the bruise with the tip of her pretty finger. "He's got the upper hand; he's so much bigger than you. You ought to fence the pell."

"Which is why I should have been able to get out of the way." Gisela laughed softly. Vivica wasn't impressed.

"It's simply barbaric of him to—" her cooing was cut short. Vivica had sat beside the bath on a bench on a ruched, velvet cushion with a chatoyant, glass orb in her lap, which to Gisela's eyes, was swirling with mysterious vapours. She had been stroking the orb while Gisela bathed, peering into it with intent. Gisela abandoned her bruises to look over her shoulder at Vivica's sudden loss of words.

"Oh, my darling," she gasped and let the crystal ball roll to the floor.

"What is it? Vivica. . ." Gisela stood in the water at the alarm in Vivica's voice, the sudden cold of the air covering her body in gooseflesh.

"It's just as I thought. Just as I thought!" The ruffling of Vivica's satin gown could be heard as she hurried down the corridor. "Rathar, open up." Vivica did not wait for a reply but rather opened the door and let herself in.

"Come in." Rathar rolled his eyes.

"You're wrong, about the Stalker in Lanthchilde, or at least you're misinformed." Vivica put her hands on her hips and sighed.

"Impossible. I was there, the whole eastern half of the city is blockaded."

"Listen, Rath, I don't know who they have, but they don't have a Stalker. I am the mistress of Borghild. I know who comes into this castle, and I know who leaves it, that is, I keep watch over all my boys, including you. There are currently thirty Stalkers alive and active which this castle has produced, and I know where each and every one of them is. Lanthchilde is not one of those places."

"You sure it's not that Adel fellow? More useless than wen-ridden bollocks, that one." Vivica gave him a rather maternal glare and sat in a wicker bottomed chair beside the bed where Rathar was lying, thinking. "Why would someone claim to be a Stalker or a Vestal, even under pains of capture and death?" He held a fist to his forehead in thought.

"What if. . . what if they aren't claiming anything?" Vivica began, "What if *someone else* has called them a Stalker and a Vestal, or even still, what if they're under a spell?"

"Why would someone want a false Stalker and a false Vestal killed; and even yet, they would have still had to murder those people in the burgages? What a right labour."

"It's not about them. It's about you." Vivica's face grew stony and still.

"Whoever it is wants to deface Stalkers and Vestals, wants them to seem dangerous and untrustworthy. Whoever did this is making life dangerous for you. Lanthchilde may just be the conception; word will spread, the lies will be exaggerated, and the truth will be twisted. It'll start to become dangerous for you no matter where you go. That may be the goal."

"Well they did a fine job. Drove me all the way back to Borghild with my head up my arse."

"You couldn't have known. I'll have to take care in looking into Mirabelle."

"Will you find things out, Viv?"

"Darling," Vivica's coloured lips twisted into a devious smile, and she batted her lashes, "I'll find out *everything*." Rathar sat up on the edge of the bed and leaned forward, taking her hands in his.

"Vivica, this could be dangerous. We might be opening something much bigger than it seems." Suddenly there was something hard, something fierce in her eyes. It sent a shudder down Rathar's spine.

"You needn't worry about me, my dear," she almost whispered.

Rathar searched her face; she looked not a day older, but somehow, she looked more weathered since his youth. He searched her face and remembered the long days of training in his youth. Running, sparring, studying. He remembered a bruised body and cracked lips. He remembered not being able to hold back the stinging tears the first time he shifted, but he remembered her holding herb scented rags to bleeding faces. He remembered being ill and being brought a compress and a mug of hot broth. The magician had always had a soft spot for the young Stalkers, but, he thought, she was not all soft. He remembered the woman that raised him and the power that she had within to rear boys into men, not just any boys, boys left to die in the mountains of Rotrude, and not just any men, Stalkers.

•• ———— ••●•• ———— ••

It was late winter when Vivica rode out for Dimia. She left the castle well protected of course, under many enchantments and spells, and, as she put it, in very capable hands.

"There is always a summit of the northwestern magicians in the Consortium in late winter; I have persuaded them to host the affair in Dimia. I have what you might call 'sway' in the matter of decision making being that I am one of the oldest and most respected magicians in the Consortium at present. If there is anything going on with Mirabelle, I want it under my nose where she is most vulnerable, most comfortable, most liable to make a mistake," she said, stepping up into the stirrup and swinging herself into the saddle with elegance.

Gisela looked at her in awe. She looked no older than thirty, but she concluded that if she was one of the oldest magicians in the Consortium, she had to be well into her hundreds. Rathar had always kept the mistress's age a secret as a sort of game.

"I'll do a bit of digging while I'm there. I'm on good terms with Mirabelle, though she knows I'm the mistress of Borghild, so if there's anything fishy going on with you, she might just hold her tongue. We'll see."

Rathar secured the saddlebags on the back of the sleek, dapple-grey mare that bore his mistress. The horse stomped and snorted, ready to take flight as if her burden were as light as a feather.

"I shall return after mid-month. Allow nobody within the walls. As I said, I'm expecting no one this winter." Her lips never twisted into a smile; she simply rode off in haste, kicking up clods of frozen mud and stinking ice behind her.

Rathar dusted the remnants off his trousers and shirtsleeves and waved her off. "We might as well train," he shrugged. "I don't see a better use of our time."

Gisela nodded.

•• ———— ••●•• ———— ••

When Vivica arrived at Dimia, she was weary, for she rode at an arduous pace. "Treat the horse well," she told the stable boy as she sauntered around the side of the towering grey walls of the castle. "She has come a long way and has worked very hard." Vivica handed over the reins and looked over her shoulder at an approaching figure in black.

"Look what the cat dragged in," came a cheerful voice, not at all matching the dark attire whence it came.

"Luanda, how I've missed you." Vivica smiled and pulled the black hood off of a slight and narrow face framed with hair icy blonde, cropped just below the ears. Her cheeks were bright and rosy, her eyes as blue as the sea; her features were almost juvenile. The two magicians embraced warmly, and Luanda patted down the creases in her black dress with long sleeves and buttons all the way up the neck. The only thing remarkable about her trappings was the giant emerald ring she bore on her right hand.

"I heard," Luanda chirruped, "that the summit which was supposed to take place in Isolde, was moved here to Dimia upon your request. Nobody batted an eye but me of course."

"That's because you know me, dear."

"You'll tell me everything, won't you?"

"Of course. In fact, I'll be needing your help. But for now, darling, tell me, how have you been?" The two walked arm in arm into the castle, chattering as they went.

•• ———— ••●•• ———— ••

The evening before the summit was a grand affair. All the magicians of the Provinces participated in a gala of sorts. It was truly something to behold, even by a magician's standards. Vivica entered the round room and gazed up into the domed ceiling which had been enchanted in honour of the season to look like billowing clouds pouring forth a gentle snowfall only without the unbearable chill. There were tables of roasted grouse, stuffed pigeons, braised tenderloins, boiled lobsters, all sorts of vegetables with broths and sauces, cranberries and apples, figs and nuts, and the wine was plentiful. If the tables weren't beautiful enough, the guests were dressed to match, and Vivica was no exception. She was accoutered in a deep emerald gown made of satin that reached the floor. It hung from her shoulders by two narrow straps and had a gathering of fabric around her breast which was pinned like a sash and fell like a waterfall down her hip, and on her hands she wore black, silk gloves that reached her elbows. She was elegant, smelling of evergreen. As Vivica looked around the room, she noticed it was clearly divided. Though most of the magicians of the northwestern provinces had come, there were clear friendships, and if what Rathar suspected was true, those friendships would mean clear divisions and loyalties. Luanda of Brangian, her closest friend, for one, was an ally she could count on. Other possible allies would be Favian of Dain and Rose of Isolde who were prattling together in the middle of the room. On the opposing side was Orien of Gundrada who had been watching her carefully from the moment she entered. Mirabelle of Dimia was close with Orien. Margaret of Derwinter was a confidant of Mirabelle—everyone knew that. And then there were those to whom loyalty had no sway such as Beatrice of Guise and Berinon of Reliquary who were circling the room and making conversation with everyone. Beatrice was an old magician in the Province and had other favourable qualities, surely Vivica would be able to appeal to her in a time of need; the only downside was that her lover, Berinon of Reliquary liked to remain neutral in all things; it would be difficult to sway his influence on her; however Orien was outgoing, an uninhibited extrovert who had earned himself the position of head of council either by favour or by fear. Whatever the affair was, this summit would ultimately go the way of him and his *lackeys*.

"Mirabelle approaches," Vivica whispered to Luanda, hooked on her elbow, "we must draw something out of her if we can."

"You must have heard the awful news. Just awful." Mirabelle approached Vivica, her eyes flashing with something that definitely wasn't sympathy. Perhaps surprise, shock even.

"I'm sorry darling, I'm not sure what you mean." Vivica remained soft and receptive, touching Mirabelle's shoulder warmly.

"In Lanthchilde, did you hear? They killed a Stalker just the other day. The poor fellow was held captive for weeks until they ended him. He massacred the city, like the stories of old. Poor training, I suppose." The last sentence was meant as a jab.

"I've heard nothing about this." Vivica furrowed her brow in feigned concern. "I'll have to look into this, certainly."

"The mistress of Borghild lives under a rock," Mirabelle said, a little too loudly and with a chuckle. "Burned at the stake. The Vestal, too, a beacon of hope who stood by and watched the whole bloody affair." She shivered with what Vivica could only be described as delight.

"You don't, by chance, know which of my Stalkers was killed, do you, Mirabelle?"

Mirabelle shrugged carelessly. "I'm afraid the name has. . . escaped me." Her voice turned sour, but her face remained lovely. "Whoever it was seemed to have gotten what was coming to him," she added. She gracefully pinched a flute of wine off of a salver as it passed and turned away, making for similar company.

"Don't worry about her." Luanda smoothed her bustling black gown that came down to her calves, overlaid with black damask and teeming with black, satin petticoats, still adorned with the massive emerald on her finger. "If what you told me was true, and I believe that it was, you have nothing to be sorry over. Everyone knows your Stalkers are guided by the best Vestals in the Provinces; and a massacre *in the city?* It hardly seems likely."

"They like women, and they like drink; it seems to be born into them—loudmouthed and loathsome at times, but by my hand they know the consequences for falling to bloodlust. Besides, I know this all to be a foul lie to begin with, and Mirabelle has given herself away already." Vivica smiled slyly and sipped a flute of wine from the salver. "She mentioned hope."

"Let Mirabelle play the fool, then." Luanda playfully jutted her elbow into Vivica's ribs. "Let's eat and drink, shall we? The summit tomorrow will be dreadfully boring, don't you think? It's best to make merry while we can."

"Of course, you're right, darling. We shall see what comes of the summit tomorrow, though. I don't think we will find it quite as boring as you think." Vivica peered over her wine glass at Orien's prying eyes.

•• ———— ••●•• ———— ••

All of the magician's at the summit shuffled into the hosting castle's great hall the next morning, some with grace, some hung over from the night before, most expecting nothing to come of the summit as was tradition; each would give a tidy summary of their work in their respective areas, the Consortium would restate its unrelenting loyalty to each other, and the magician's would be on their way.

"I suppose," Mirabelle started with a small cough, "I suppose seeing that we have decided to hold this such summit in Dimia, that I shall speak first."

"No." Orien held up a proud, wizened hand. "The summit will discuss, before the posts of its various magicians, another topic which has become the chief reason for this gathering today."

The magicians looked around at each other; Mirabelle smiled slightly.

Chapter

06

G ISELA STOOD IN THE COURTYARD and turned her face into her shoulder against the cold breeze. She placed her finger on the grey, withered branch that jutted out of the plum tree, crusted over with frozen snow. Gently, she twisted her fingers around the branch, half expecting a green sprout to appear, but there was nothing. She sighed and returned inside where Rathar was sitting in front of the fire, now orange and red and made by human hands, buried in a book titled, *Cartography of the Northeastern Provinces by Lord Crewe of Guise.*

"Rath. . . do you hear that?"

"Hear what?" Rathar didn't look up from the book, a strange and rare moment to see him so captivated and off his guard.

"Hooves."

Rathar shut the book and stood up. Indeed, there was the sound of hooves sloshing up the icy pathway before the great doors to the castle. Rathar bounded up the stairs to the tower that overlooked the doors.

"Look there," he whispered to Gisela, who had followed him, but was catching up and catching her breath, "he presents the crimson banner. He's a Stalker."

"Rathar, Vivica was clear. She said not to let anyone in."

"Yes, but. . ." He pinched his stubbled cheeks, "he's one of us."

"Does he look familiar?"

Rathar thought for a moment to himself, and his face looked decisive. "The Stalkers I was raised with were children when we were together. Our paths don't often cross as men; only a handful do I know well, but this is not a familiar face."

"I don't know. . ." Gisela started but was interrupted by Rathar.

"State your name," he called out from the tower.

"I am Merek, I am here to see the mistress of Borghild. I present the crimson banner; please allow me entrance." *Polite*, he thought.

"Is Merek a name from your youth?" Gisela whispered.

Rathar was quiet for a moment, then without hesitation he leapt up from his spot in the tower. "Yes. I have heard of Merek, though we were not of the same cohort." He ran back down the stairs to open the great oak doors. "Welcome, Merek, I am familiar with your reputation, yet we are not yet properly acquainted." Rathar smiled and clapped Merek firmly on the shoulder. He pointed towards Merek's horse. "Long ride, was it?"

"Fuck," Merek replied, pulling his wool cloak tight around his shoulders. "It's damned cold out; you have no idea how glad

I am to be here. Say, take my horse to the stable and point me toward the mistress, won't you?" *There's that typical Stalker charm,* Rathar thought.

"Gisela, take this horse to the stable, I'll show Merek inside." Gisela nodded quickly and took the horse by the reins, shivering outside of the warmth of the castle. "I'm afraid if you're looking for Vivica, you've come at an unfortunate time. She's occupied with an errand and won't be back for a while."

"How long is a while?"

"I'm not sure exactly, but I can see you to a room in the castle for now. It'll be good to catch up, Merek." Rathar smiled, more from the warmth of the castle than anything, and led Merek inside. "You'll find the room may be small, but comfortable. . . and nostalgic."

"Just like I remember." Merek grinned, slumping down his saddlebags into the wicker chair beside the bed. He reached down and patted the thin, straw mattress knocking on the planks below. "Right, comfortable," he jested.

"It's better than the forest floor in the crux of winter." Rathar smiled and Merek agreed heartily. "Come, dry your boots by the fire; it's nothing like Vivica's fires, but it's warm enough."

"I have to check that a few of my more fragile possessions managed the journey, then I'll be right there."

Rathar grunted in affirmation and walked down the corridor. "Sela." Rathar grabbed Gisela's arm as she leaned over the fire in the great hall, red cheeked and still shivering from the cold. "Sit next to me. You know how they can be." He was whispering. She nodded in compliance, and when Merek appeared in the hall and took a seat beside the fire, Gisela dragged a stool opposite their guest and sat next to Rathar.

"Your friend is shy." Merek teased.

"You seem to lack the company of a friend." Rathar was serious.

"Oh, nothing to worry about, nothing to worry about. She's back in Reliquary visiting her sisters while I run an errand here to Borghild. I figure this land is wild enough; there's really no need for her good company. I intend to pick her up once my errand is complete."

"What's her name, might I ask?" Gisela chirruped quietly, "In case I know her, just out of curiosity."

"Jocosa." Merek smiled. "She does her job, but she is not the rare beauty that I see before me, if I may be bold enough to say. I wonder how Rathar gets any work done." Merek laughed heartily. Gisela looked down at her feet in embarrassment.

"No. You may not be bold enough to say," Rathar snarled. "Now, what errand brings you to the mistress of Borghild?"

"That's private, I'm afraid."

"Fair enough." The rest of the evening consisted of other such vague statements about childhood and work, and gently prying questions until Merek decided it was high time that he turn in for the night.

"I think I'll stay until the coals dim," Rathar said over politely.

"As you wish. I'll see you in the morning. I would kiss your hand, pretty thing, if I wasn't worried of losing my teeth." He laughed dryly and faded down the corridor.

For a while Gisela and Rathar sat silently watching the fire die, probably, Gisela thought, waiting for Merek to fall asleep.

Once the coals were sufficiently dampened, Gisela leaned into the hearth and lit the flame of a tall tapered candle in a brass dish.

"Rathar." She spoke softly, shadows dancing across her face. "I don't know what you're up to."

"Go to my room tonight. Sleep there. I'll come once I'm done thinking."

"But. . . don't you. . . don't you know how that will look?" Gisela stammered, feeling her cheeks turn red and hot.

"I know exactly how it will look. Do as I say."

Gisela swallowed hard. She trusted Rathar fully, but to a Vestal, the image of modesty was of salient importance; Merek had already made suggestions, and she didn't want to confirm them. She nodded and made her way quietly down the corridor toward Rathar's room.

•• ——— ••●•• ——— ••

Gisela waited up for Rathar for what felt like, to her, an age. She fiddled with her sleeve, cursing herself for wearing a snug, cerulean gown lined with white mink. Vivica had left it for Gisela, praising its merits for holding warmth, but now she found herself missing the familiar layers of wheaten robes that typically masked her figure. When Rathar entered the room, he was silent and the only thing that gave him away was his shadow that crossed before the ever dying light in the brass dish beside his bed. Gisela sat, hugging her knees, trying to keep her nodding head aloft as sleep threatened to take her.

"Why are you still awake?" Rathar whispered, silently closing the door behind him as he entered.

"Why am I here?" she challenged. There was something in her voice and a choking in her throat.

Rathar took up the candle in the dish and held it up to Gisela's face. "We sleep in the same room all the time," he said blithely; he was trying to pacify her in his own way.

"Not like this! You *mean* for him to see me leave this room tomorrow." She choked and another tear spilled down her cheek. She hastily wiped it away with the mink on her sleeve.

"I know what bothers you, Sela. But the question of your virtue will never leave these walls. I swear it. Now sleep." Rathar blew out the candle and leaned back into the wicker chair. Gisela buried her face into her knees and cried until sleep overcame her.

•• ———— ••●•• ———— ••

Morning had left Gisela more hardened than the night before. Rathar had instructed her to wait to come out of the room until after him. She obeyed, shuffling between her feet. She looked herself up and down and decided as long as this filthy lie was to go on, she would not sully her Vestal's robes, and so decided to remain in Vivica's gowns until Merek was to take his leave. Gisela told herself that with pride, peering out the window and clicking her tongue impatiently. As soon as a reasonable length of time had passed, she prayed, signed herself with a spiritual gesture, and slipped out into the corridor.

•• ———— ••●•• ———— ••

Merek did not hide his opinion when Gisela emerged into the great hall; though he wasn't brave enough to speak and pass verbal judgement, he made no effort to conceal his brazen expressions. Gisela looked down, away, anywhere to avoid thawing her hardened exterior into tears again.

"Why don't you take breakfast in the chancery?" Rathar handed a plate of bread, cheese, and dried figs to Gisela who happily and silently obliged.

"Let us train today, Merek. You must have the itch as I do, to move; sitting around this castle all day just won't cut it."

"Excellent idea. What do you have in mind?"

"A bit of fencing could be lively." Rathar smiled with his lips, but his eyes were of ice. Merek agreed and the two walked down a long corridor that brought them to a well-kept yard that had obviously been imposed by magic, for it did not belong in the swamp at all. The foreground was a thick, plush lawn with a gravel walking path along the border, outlined with rows of tall hedges and imposing cedars. Beyond that was a glasshouse that contained a flourishing herb garden. The yard, however, was battered here and there from sliding, slashing, and previous contending. Merek looked around at the little battlefield slightly surprised.

"Not as delicate as she looks." Rathar smiled. "Go ahead. You draw first." Rathar and Merek settled themselves opposite each other, and Merek reached across with his right hand and drew his blade. Rathar mirrored him and in an instant, the clashing of metal rang out across the yard and sparks flew between the two men. Merek swung upwards from his waist, but the movement was too obvious, and Rathar deflected him with an overhead strike that knocked Merek off balance. Rathar took the moment of upset to slash from his left shoulder across, but where Merek lacked in physical strength, he made up for in speed; he ducked out of the way, spun around and slashed sideways. He was, however, not as quick as Rathar, something Rathar found peculiar. Rathar met him with another brawny block which almost knocked Merek off his feet, but he glided by luck on his toes and managed to stay standing. The two spun and crossed blades sending a shower of sparks between their faces, and for a few minutes the match seemed even, but in the end, in a battle of strength and speed, Rathar had the upper hand; the two crossed blades near the chest and Rathar pressed in with his advantage, forcing Merek to the ground, holding the point of his sword against Merek's navel. Merek, Rathar noticed, apart from having a cut lip and visibly trembling, was out of breath and desperately trying to hide it.

"A good warm up." Rathar lifted his blade and offered his hand.

"Perhaps that is enough for now." Merek took Rathar's hand and stood, still breathing heavily, and looking a bit pale, fearing for a moment Rathar might really kill him.

The two walked back into the castle, Merek mopping the sweat from his brow with the back of his sleeve. "Isn't there any blasted ale in this place? Good, durum ale?"

"I'm afraid the mistress prefers wine to beer, but you knew that. I'm going to find Gisela for a moment." Rathar began walking toward the chancery.

"Best not to get tangled up with womenfolk, Rathar," Merek shouted after him, tenderly touching his cut lip and pouring himself some wine into a crystal goblet. "They're all the same. First, they prefer wine to ale, then they prefer your purse to theirs. They're good for a night, maybe two. Leave it at that. No woman is worth more. Especially not that dewy eyed, canoness of yours. Take that as a little advice, brother to brother." Merek sat himself on one of the stools and kicked off his boots beside the fire, still wiping the sweat from his face, showing off a toothy grin.

A spark inside Rathar flared up, in what could only appropriately be described as rage, and he wanted nothing more in that moment than to take Merek by a handful of hair and knock his teeth in, but he remained, on the outside, impeccably temperate. "You, brother, have been duped. It would seem you've not known a single woman in your lifetime for they are fair and noble creatures. One can only conclude you've been sleeping with men. . . or dwarves."

Rathar smiled and walked down the corridor leaving Merek fuming and cursing and throwing his boots. Rathar entered the chancery and turned the key in the lock behind him. Gisela was there waiting, leaning against a desk. She'd not touched her plate and she looked slightly ashamed but largely more concerned.

"I've done what you asked. This morning, after I came out of your room, I went to Merek's room, and I checked his bags for what he called his 'more fragile possessions.' "

"What did you find, Sela?"

"Did he say anything about us?"

"Gisela, what was in the bags?"

"Yes, I'm sorry, that's of greater import. Rathar, there were tinctures of twining vine, some strong spirit, and. . . well, I can't believe people still believe in these sorts of fables but. . . a glass dagger."

"A glass dagger. Highly superstitious people still think it is the only way to kill a magician, to pierce the heart with a glass dagger. They say to slay a magician by a common alloy will only bring about a reincarnation. I guess the poison is to immobilize her."

"Rathar, why would Merek, a Stalker, want to kill Vivica, the mistress of Borghild? She raised you both."

"Because Merek isn't a Stalker." Rathar pursed his lips. "He's not the meticulous sort, so I don't think he'll know you went through his things, but be on your guard tonight."

"How did he find Borghild?" Gisela gasped.

"I don't know, Sela, but he cannot leave it. We risk the secrecy of this place and the safety of Vivica."

Gisela did not know what that meant, but she felt frightened.

●● ——— ●●●●● ——— ●●

Merek and Rathar had been sitting opposite each other in relative silence and contempt while Gisela made quiet conversation with Rathar about this and that odd job they could do once winter had released its icy grasp on the Provinces, and such and such an acquaintance they could visit once the deepest snows had receded from the pass of Rotrude.

"You must know," Merek said after a while, "must have some idea when the mistress of this castle will return."

"I'm afraid she gave no time of return," Rathar lied.

Merek clicked his tongue and adjusted his belt, sighing audibly. "Clearly I have offended you, Rathar," Merek said after a while. "And such a thing should not stand between such old friends."

"Certainly not," agreed Rathar with a smile that could only be described as forced.

"Fuck all." Merek threw his hands into his lap. "Since the mistress of Borghild is away for such a length, I will take my leave in the morning for I have things I must attend to, but until then let us reconcile. I have with me a draught of particular quality." He winked. "I've been saving it for a special occasion. Even for the fair and noble creature." The words were exaggerated almost in jest. "Only let me retrieve it from my things." Merek stood and hobbled to his room with their goblets, already tipsy from the amount of wine he'd drunk, and Gisela and Rathar looked at each other with knowing apprehension. When Merek had returned, he handed each of his companions a goblet and toasted to their good health, draining his own goblet in one hasty go. "It's best to do it one lick, strong stuff you know." He laughed unpleasantly. "Go on." He urged, this time without smiling. Gisela stood and threw a log into the fire with her free hand. "What's that now, I'm only trying to make amends. Drink! Drink to your good health and your. . . prepossessing looks!" he hiccoughed.

Gisela looked at Rathar, and her stomach sank as she watched Rathar pat his boot and look at her with calm eyes. Nausea overtook her and she didn't know if she could move a pounce.

"Indeed, Merek." Rathar was calm as a still sea, but he slapped his boot in enthusiasm and pressed the goblet to his lips.

Gisela understood at once what she was to do. She reached over to Merek's boots still standing by the fire and pulled the wrapped hilt of a shining dagger out, and in one swift movement she dropped her crystal goblet to the floor, shattering it into a hundred glistening shards, and reached around, plunging the dagger swiftly into Merek's chest. For a moment he was still, but then he convulsed, grabbing her arm, tightly at first, but then slowly relinquishing as the warmth spilled down over Gisela's lap. She hastily pushed his weight off of her as he sputtered through his final breaths. Rathar threw the contents of his goblet into the fire and let his head fall back, sighing in relief, but he was interrupted by spasming sobs. He bent down and picked up Merek by handfuls of his tunic and rather rudely tossed him aside, then crouching there he embraced Gisela not knowing if the warmth seeping through his clothes was blood or tears.

"I killed. . . I killed Merek," she sobbed.

"You did not kill Merek."

"I've never killed. . . killed a man. . . before."

"You did well, Sela." Rathar stroked her golden hair now sticky with blood, trying to remember what it had felt like to kill his first man. It had been at the battle of Garburh; many men had fallen by his sword, and he had been almost in a trance. It was not accompanied by such emotion, for compassion and feeling had always been Gisela's realm and ruling.

"I don't want. . . I don't want to do well. . . Rath. . . never again." It was one thing to kill river-shrews and were-dogs and harpies and other such beasts of the wild, but to kill a person. . . Gisela choked on her tears and could not be consoled for some time, so Rathar held her there until the fire grew quite cold.

"Are you done crying?" he asked. "I've made you cry for many days now, and if you're done, I don't intend to do so anymore." He lifted her up to her feet, and she rubbed her swollen eyes with crusty hands. "Go change and get some sleep. Leave that dress outside your door. I'll burn it with the body." Gisela nodded and walked sullenly down the corridor to her room, cursing her tears for Rathar had always admonished them, but in this instance his tenderness had prevailed. Rathar fought the urge to punch out the teeth of the dead man on the floor.

Chapter

07

"THE CONSORTIUM," ORIEN BEGAN, "WILL be cleansed." Immediately chatter erupted amongst the gathered magicians. There was arguing, hostility, and general noise until Berinon called for silence and order.

"It has been brought to the attention of the Consortium that half of our Provinces operate quite differently than the other half."

"Damned factions," Rose of Isolde spat at the feet of Mirabelle, and Favian had to restrain her. Mirabelle haughtily stuck her nose in the air.

"What do you mean *cleansed*?" Luanda warbled, and the magicians nodded their heads eager for an explanation.

"If your name is called, you will step down and live a life in peace outside the Consortium, or I will personally spill your blood at this table." Orien's eyes were glinting, hard, hungry almost.

"Who decided?" Vivica asked what most were thinking. "Who decided who was worthy?"

"The decision," Beatrice remained undisturbed, "was not uninformed."

"Who has Reliquary?" Vivica shot a glare at the ever-prying eyes of Orien whose smile only vexed her.

•• ———— ••●•• ———— ••

Gisela had kept mostly to her room, morose for days, and Rathar took the opportunity to make ready to leave. They had stayed, he decided, in the clasp of Borghild for long enough and he was craving normalcy, especially for Gisela's sake. Besides, Borghild was no longer as safe as they had hoped. He knocked softly at her door. She was dressed once more in her long, wheaten Vestal's robes, folding up parcels and packing them neatly into saddlebags. "I saw you preparing; I followed suit," she mumbled.

"It's time we left this place. The buds will spring forth any week now. Though the pass hasn't fully melted, we can go back down south and around. We'll be careful. Besides, the land is in friendly hands."

"Are you sure we shouldn't wait for Vivica to return? What if she has information?"

"I'd like to get moving. These summits are usually uneventful. What she found out was most likely drivel, and anyway, she knows how to find me."

Gisela screwed up her face in contemplation but did not argue. "I trust you, Rath," she finally chirruped, quietly, and turned back to her folding and packing.

"You'll feel better." He smiled and squeezed her shoulder. "Once we're gone from this place."

•• ——— ••●•• ——— ••

Vivica returned to Borghild in the first days of spring at a brisk pace. She bounded off her horse gracefully and threw open the castle doors at once with a wave of her hands and a gale force. The halls were cold and barren. The hearth was empty and full of dead ash. The air reeked of old blood. She was spattered in crimson.

•• ——— ••●•• ——— ••

"I could get used to horses." Rathar smiled and glanced over his shoulder at Gisela and Lief ambling along behind.

"I thought you'd be complaining of more mouths to feed." Gisela smirked.

"Apart from the ache in my arse, I must admit that my feet are enjoying the recess. They'd be a treat on the roads where the ground is hard."

"We'd better get connected to a main road soon," Gisela said. "We need to fill our purse, and there are a few Temples between here and Reliquary." They trotted on for days along the byways making their way to the main road that would take them through inhabited places, camping by night in the woods that framed their path. Spring was beginning to show itself like a shy lover in glances and glimpses, here a peek of fresh green grass under the blanket of dead leaves, there a sprouting bud on the end of what looked like a dead and ragged branch. The elements of winter had not been terribly harsh in the bosom of Borghild, but it had been trying all the same, and now spring brought with it a warmth to beat upon the backs of the travellers, giving them optimism anew.

"Rath?" Gisela and Leif halted behind Rathar, sitting up in the saddle inhaling deeply. "What is it?"

"There is a town up ahead if memory serves me right. Not too far away. Adonica."

"Why did we stop?"

"Because we are about to earn our purse." Rathar grinned and his nostrils flared. He jumped nimbly off of his unnamed horse and handed the reins to Gisela. "Find somewhere safe, you know what to do," Rathar growled as the grotesque and flaming wound-like colours pulsed down his face, neck, and arms. Gisela nodded. Find somewhere safe, and stay out of the way; that was everything she could do. As Gisela peeked from behind a cluster of tall stone slabs, she saw frost slowly creeping and spreading across the ground like a disease. It was a Notos, an aspirmeyg that fought with ice. The beast was enormous and fearsome looking with curling, sharp claws covered in chunks of thick ice. It let out a shrieking scream and icy daggers, wispy looking, but very tangible to Rathar shot forth from the beast's jaws. Rathar rolled onto his right shoulder to avoid them, and he drew the long, bronze sword from his side, slashing toward the belly of the massive creature and missing by a foot. The Notos swung its arms sending masses of cloudy ice flying, missing Rathar by inches as he dodged with skill, swinging his blade. Suddenly, the Notos lunged forth in a motion unexpected and drove its icy claws into the ground, sending creeping frost and ice across the road and up the Rathar's legs; he was frozen where he stood and astonished, yanking his legs in alarm. He looked to his left where his bronze blade stuck out of the ground, frozen at a jagged angle; the Notos lugged its massive form forward and raised its cumbersome arm to strike the Stalker. It swung with strength and sharp claws bared, but howled and screeched in pain as its arm fell to the ground beside it in a wispy pool of purple blood. Rathar's eyes were wide in shock, and perhaps the beast's were wider yet in fear. Before Rathar, still frozen, stood Gisela holding the bronze blade she had wielded from her own side, a replica of the Stalker's sword lest her companion should ever lose his own; it was she that had braced herself before the Notos and cut off its arm, and she wasn't finished. She lunged forward, taking advantage of the beast's stupefaction, and plunged the blade into its hip as she couldn't reach any higher. It was enough to drop the Notos to its knees, and without a second thought Gisela swung the blade with skill around and lopped the head of her adversary from its shoulders, something she had seen Rathar do many times over. Blood pooled at her feet, and the frost and ice which had covered the makeshift battleground immediately began to recede. Gisela stooped down and ran her fingers through the purple pool. It stuck to them, not a wisping dream but a sticky sap. Her breathing was even and calm. For a while she and Rathar stood in the road without speaking, but only trying to understand what was happening.

"Rathar," Gisela finally whispered. "I. . . I can't see. Come here." Rathar slowly came before her, grasping her wrists as she felt for his face and placed her thumbs on his grown-over eyes. She could feel the thick tissue recede from his eyelids, and as it did, the darkness from her own eyes began to fade as well revealing the forest around them and the road before them, but not without leaving behind a splitting pain in her head and the feeling that all of her body was on fire. Suddenly, Gisela heaved a tremendous sigh. "Rath! I don't know. . . I couldn't see! Just. . . the smell. . . I was scared for you, I didn't think! I just did it because. . . how did I do it?" Rathar said nothing. He was still holding her wrists, looking at her face smattered with purple blood, no closer to understanding what had just happened than she was. "What I did, it was impossible, right? Rathar? I'm just a Vestal. Aspirmeygs. . . they can't, I can't. . . Rath?" Gisela was pleading now and holding her head in her hands. Rathar shook his head.

"You saved my life."

"No." Gisela blushed. *I don't need you anyway.* The words echoed in her mind again. She was unsteady on her feet now from the pain that wracked every part of her.

"I don't know how you did it, but you did it. And there's your proof." He pointed at the bloody mound before them, and hoisted Gisela up by the shoulder. "Shifting. . . it's a pain in the arse," he mumbled and led her to the horses.

•• —— ••●•• —— ••

The ride to Adonica seemed painfully drawn out, and both Rathar and Gisela were silent in thought until reaching their destination. The mood lightened, however, as they approached their first Temple in some time. "Finally, somewhere where someone is not trying to kill us. . . or curse us. . . or worse." Rathar growled.

"Worse?" Gisela's eyes widened.

"I can certainly think of worse." He clicked his tongue and tapped his heels into his horse's ribs, urging it on between two sizeable stanchions which held between them a wooden archway that welcomed them to Adonica. They rode through the unsurfaced streets, splashing hooves through mucky puddles which had just clearly welcomed rain, and Rathar noticed that the smell was not altogether unpleasant. The people weren't unfriendly either as a small gathering stopped Gisela asking her for a blessing to which she happily obliged them. The irony was not lost on Rathar that the crowd had stopped them outside a brothel. He chuckled to himself, but stopped when one of the cathouse girls blew him a kiss and looked him up and down slowly. He looked at his feet; he looked at a bird in a tree; he looked anywhere and everywhere to avoid meeting her gaze, but he had seen her. She was beautiful, soaking wet, a bit muddy at the hems of her skirts, and her eyes were smeared with kohl without the slightest finesse, but there was a beauty behind what had run her ragged. *Finally,* the blessings and orisons were done with, and Rathar and Gisela mounted their horses once more to make for the Temple.

"Hey, fire-beard," the woman called after Rathar, "you know where to find me, sweeting." She giggled. Rathar blushed.

"Do you. . . know her?" Gisela raised a brow. She had never seen such colour in Rathar's face before.

"Don't be ridiculous." Rathar rolled his eyes. They rode toward the small stable beside the Temple. Inside the Temple was as much at home as the Stalker ever felt. They were all more or less the same. A great roaring fire kept a light in the middle of the room in a squared off pit with cocottes and spits for common use and benches to dry your boots and socks. Straw-stuffed cots lined the walls in pairs where Stalkers and Vestals could rest in relative comfort and safety for free; and what a Temple lacked in privacy it made up for in payment. Once a month, if they were roaming the area, each Stalker and Vestal pair was entitled to visit the ledger-man and receive their payment for keeping the people safe from aspirmeygs, a collected tax on the people of the Temple's town. It was a modest sum, but it was enough. Rathar dropped his pack and saddlebags on the red, glazed tile floor beside a cot in the furthest corner of the room and sat down in a crunch of flinders; there was just one other Stalker and Vestal pair in the Temple, and they weren't familiar. *Excellent*, Rathar mused to himself, *no need for blasted small talk.*

"I'm going out." Gisela dropped her pack beside Rathar's and pulled the hood of her cloak over her head in case of a further drizzle. Rathar said nothing, neither did he look up. He only struck a bit of spark-stone over his carved, red wooden pipe and began to puff silently with eyes closed and arms crossed. "I'll leave you to brood then." She rolled her eyes and turned on her heel out from the Temple and into the streets of the Adonica. It was a quaint town with a moderately-sized market and a Temple at least. The ledger-man had paid a decent amount of silver; they were nowhere near recovering the amount Rathar had spent at the apothecary, but they could buy food or a room if need be, and that was a relief, especially considering that Gisela's Vestal's dowry was spent now. She had thought that in a pinch they could sell Leif or the pack pony, but she had grown rather attached. Browsing the market seemed to take Gisela's mind off the burden that laid there for a while. Barrels of vegetables and salted meats. Herbs in baskets blended and filled the air with the smells of mint, rosemary, and. . . a sweet, familiar scent. Gisela turned her nose up to the air and smelled again a hint of something lovely. Out of the corner of her eye she spotted it; there on the side of the walking path had sprouted a small clump of snowdrops. She smiled and bent down to pick them, tying them delicately into a bouquet with a white ribbon she pulled from her hair.

•• —————— ••●•• —————— ••

"What's this?" Rathar smiled, his eyes still closed. "Snowdrops."

"How can you smell them behind all that smoke?" Gisela jested. She had crouched down as silently as possible and placed the little bouquet on Rathar's chest. "I'm a Stalker." He grumbled and inhaled sharply through his nose. "What. . ." Rathar began, "what do you smell?"

"Don't worry." Gisela shook her head. "I can't smell the flowers. All I smell is your pipe." She breathed deeply to make sure. Rathar looked relieved, though he attempted to hide it.

"They please me." He grinned, "Overcoming challenges. That's the meaning behind a snowdrop." He placed them atop his pack before putting out his pipe in a small bowl in the corner, taking care not to squash the delicate petals. Without another word he rolled over onto his cot and closed his eyes to the glow of the fire. *Your burdens are heavier than ever,* Gisela thought as she sunk down into her own cot beside him, *but you always could sleep well in a Temple.* Rathar slowed his breathing and listened for sleep to overcome Gisela. When he was sure that she could not be easily stirred, he stood silently, pulled his cloak around his shoulders, and stole into the darkness of Adonica. He hadn't been to Adonica in a long time, but the streets were well laid out in clean grids. For a moment he stood at an intersection and peered down the damp street at the brothel, dimly lit with thick clouds of incense pouring out of one of the open windows, and he felt some strange desire for the kohl smeared eyes that had so thoroughly picked him apart earlier in the day, torn by something submerged deep within to be made vulnerable. Stalkers lived a lonely life, but it shouldn't have bothered him. He came from a race unhindered by the paltry sentiments of love. Wights reproduced for efficiency; and Stalkers fooled around for mere pleasures that Vestals could not provide; Rathar, however, had always found himself uninterested in getting mixed up in the fleeting amusements of whores and the financial affairs of inequitable bawds. He felt, too, that Gisela might look on him with disappointment, might see him with unbearable shame. He couldn't bear the thought, so he shook his head and rid his mind of such a fancy, forcefully pushing the beautiful eyes from his memory. He had work to do, and in less than an hour he'd found what he was looking for, the local diviner. Diviners, Rathar thought, were mostly useless salesmen of cheap tricks. They weren't magicians with any power; they were born with the ability for magic but never honed their skills at the Magical Consortium Guild School for one reason or another, so they settled with spilling entrails and casting bone runes, all lacklustre skills to satisfy the superstition of dullards and get a bit of silver; procuring silver, that was one thing all magicians seemed to have in common; however, the one thing diviners did have were crystal balls, and in the right hands a crystal ball was a lifeline.

"There it goes again," Rathar grumbled, "I spend money as soon as I have it these days." He dropped a few silver coins into the diviner's outstretched hand, too many silver coins in his opinion, and closed the door behind him for a bit of privacy in the next room littered with crystal balls. He chose one of shining ebony with a yellow cat's eye in the middle and placed his hand on top of it muttering an incantation he had perfected from Vivica in his youth. The incantation, if properly done, with a true crystal ball, would allow communication with another ball via a phrenic connection; crystal balls were almost things of feeling and sentiment; true, there was an incantation, a formula, but in order to make a fellow appear on the other side, whether to communicate or to peer through like a window, there had to be a connection with the object in question that was almost emotional. Rathar continued muttering and stared deeply into the yellow cat's eye until slowly it began to take the form of a woman with dark lips and violet hair.

"Rathar," she said sternly, "I have been waiting."

"I know," he said in a hushed tone. "I had to find a diviner."

"There is much to tell you about the Consortium, Rath. Also, who did you kill? You left him all over my floor." Vivica's face twisted in displeasure.

"Right. . . there is much to share, too."

"Let me go first." Rathar nodded in approval but motioned with his hand for her to keep her voice down. "Rathar. . . the Consortium has been cleansed."

"What do you mean?" Rathar's voice grew slightly urgent.

"The Consortium. . . we are no longer a cohesive organization, rather many magicians are dead now, and the north has been given to a new organization of magicians, Rathar."

"I don't take your meaning by 'new' organization."

"I think you do, darling. They claim they want to try a new way. . . of magic. Rumours are going around that it's black magic, some say it's all just political factions. . . I don't know. The truth is, nobody actually really said specifically. . ."

"But the north, Viv, that's Reliquary."

"Yes. Rathar, Reliquary isn't safe for you."

"Vivica. . . who resides in Reliquary now? Is it no longer the old codger, Bernion?"

"Orien has been moved from Gundrada to Reliquary."

"Son of a bitch," Rathar growled deeply. "We can't just walk in!"

"I know, which is why I think, well, I think that Gisela should go alone."

Rathar sucked in his breath and pinched the bridge of his nose. "I can't let her go."

"She's perfectly capable of taking care of herself."

"More than you know! Viv. . . she. . . she shifted."

"She what?" Vivica leaned closer to her crystal ball as if she couldn't hear.

"She. . . she shifted. She shifted and she killed an aspirmeyg."

"Rathar, we don't have time for jesting. We need to get Gisela in and out of Reliquary, and as for you—"

"Vivica." Rathar's voice was firm and commanding. "I didn't give all my money to a fool who sells bird guts to tell farmers it's raining to joke with you. Gisela shifted, and I don't know what to do. Tell me what to do." He was pleading. He didn't often plead. To Rathar, she was the wisest and most capable person he knew, and if she didn't have a plan, he was entirely unsure who would.

"You need a magician to examine you, but I can't come right now. . ." she paused. "Who did you kill in my dining room? I told you not to let anyone in."

"Someone impersonating Merek."

"But my dear, Merek has been dead for months. His Vestal was returned to Reliquary last harvest. Did *you* know he was an imposter?"

"From the minute he waved his banner. It was a fake. He very well thought it was good enough from a distance. Though, I still haven't figured out how he managed to *find* Borghild in the first place. . ."

"Why did he come?"

"He came to kill you, Viv." Both Rathar and Vivica were silent for a time. "Why didn't Orien kill you at the summit, too?"

"He sends a sneak in the night because he knows he could never overcome me face to face my dear." Vivica smiled weakly.

"We cannot fight this battle alone, Rathar. I've my own battles now, too. I'll be in touch. Stay where you are and keep to the shadows. Both of you." Vivica emphasized her final words, and her image in the crystal ball faded back into the yellow cat's eye. Rathar sighed and pulled his cloak over his head, heeding the orders of his mistress. When he arrived back at the Temple, Gisela was still asleep where he had left her, and he laid back onto his cot comfortably, feeling sleep start to take him sooner than he had anticipated. He always could sleep well in a Temple.

•• ———— ••●•• ———— ••

"Today, we bathe!" Gisela grinned, dropping a silver coin into Rathar's hand. "We smell of horses now; it's new, but not necessarily nice."

"I agree." Rathar turned his head and sniffed himself. "Sela, don't do anything. . . apparent." Gisela twisted her face quizzically.

"Rath, I'm just taking a bath. I'm not really sure what you expect me to get up to." She laughed as she walked away down the road leaving Rathar to his concerns. He still didn't know how to tell her about Reliquary; it would break her heart to know that her sisters whom she doted on and the home which she had such an affection for was under the thumb of an enemy, but for now he supposed the best course of action was to let her laugh. It was a sound he treasured. Gisela walked into the bath and inhaled the scent of steaming thyme. She thought of the herbed baths that Vivica used to run for her as she removed her Vestal's robes and looked over the bruises on her shins and arms she'd received from the flying ice of the Notos. Ice that should have gone through her like a venomous mist. Her mind went from Vivica to Merek and the warm blood that spilled down her arm. She remembered how easy it had been to cut through him. She thought it would have been harder to do, so she had put extra strength behind the motion, but it was so easy, like a hot pie, he split open and spilled out. Gisela shuddered, and she wished for a moment to be back in her robes and not to feel so exposed, so vulnerable like Merek had been. She shook her head, letting her long, golden hair fall from the ribbons she'd used to hold it back from her face and lowered herself into the fragrant water full of chattering women.

"You mind?" A beautiful ebony-skinned woman looking to be no older than herself stepped into the pool next to Gisela. "It's a bit crowded, and I don't like to sit next to the old dodders. They just gossip." Gisela didn't have time to respond; the woman splashed herself down and began ladling water over her shoulders with a small wooden bowl. "Yikes, look at you. Your man beat you?" Then the woman caught sight of her brown robes. "Oh. Vestal? Thrilling." She said in a tone that sounded as if she meant entirely the opposite. She began gently scrubbing the black plaits

in her hair. "I mean, some people say it's a fool's life really. Looking after a feral dog on a chain all the time." She ladled the water over her head. "Boring. Me? I live a real life. No feral dogs. No chains. And no babies. That's the other thing you can be as a woman, you know, you can make babies. Not me. Boring." Gisela smiled and held out her hand. "Oh, I'm Quilla," the woman said, shaking her hand enthusiastically.

"Gisela." They both stood and shivered in the cold air. "No dogs. No chains. No babies." She added with a wink.

"Sure!" Quilla scoffed. "I'd like to meet this Stalker of yours, then! I'll believe it when I see it."

•• —— ••●•• —— ••

"I can't believe it!" Quilla sat agape, legs lazily sprawled out in an unladylike fashion, but then she wore men's clothing so it wasn't too ill suited. Rathar politely filled her cup with more ale and passed the bread toward her. "You don't bite then, Stalker? You're not gonna kill me if you swat a fly?"

Rathar smiled lightly. "No."

"Well Gisela. You're right. No dogs. No chains. But I don't know about babies. . ." Quilla squeezed one of Rathar's biceps quite forwardly. "Is that even biologically possible?" Quilla glanced at Rathar's codpiece unabashedly and Gisela blushed. Rathar rolled his eyes slightly.

"Quilla, your company has been, well, entertaining among other things. But tell us, what do you do?" Rathar poured himself another ale anticipating. Quilla looked around before leaning in and motioning for her companions to do the same.

"Hitman." She grinned a toothy grin. "That's right, friends, I live the ultimate adventure. You need a man down? I'm for hire. Only the bad ones, of course. I'm not stupid after all, and I'm a woman, so I have a heart. But, shit, I'm no girl. I travel this wide-open world, I live the ultimate adventure, and I serve the ultimate cause."

"You're unarmed," Rathar observed.

"Can't walk around armed like I am in the wild. I have to cache my stuff outside of towns or else they'll think I'm an outlaw. But don't worry, Stalker." Quilla whipped out a silver dagger from seemingly nowhere. "I'm always prepared." She let out a great laugh from her belly that didn't quite fit her beautiful, delicate features and threw back the rest of her ale. "You think I can stay here tonight, with you? Haven't found anywhere else otherwise. I just got to Adonica today. How do these Stalker's Temples work anyway?"

"Technically, no, you're not allowed, but the only other pair of Stalker and Vestal left this morning, so I don't see why not, just for a night." Gisela smiled warmly. Rathar smiled as well but flashed his eyes coldly at Gisela.

"Sela." Rathar stood and stretched casually. "Help me feed the horses before we turn in." Gisela could feel his eyes on her back all the way to the stable. Suddenly Rathar turned on his heel, shooting daggers. "I send you off; I tell you not to do anything. . . anything stupid! And you *bring home an assassin.* After everything we've been through!"

"Rath, she's—"

"She's *dangerous*, Gisela. People are trying to kill us. And you've gone and invited a murderer to bed in the only safe haven we have left."

"Rathar, I think she's on our side."

"If you tell me she is a pious woman, I'll tell you to eat shit after I remove the dagger from your back that she'll likely put there in your sleep."

"She is! God is with her! I can sense it."

"Well where is he now? Where is he when even Reliquary is in the pits?"

"He was there when you were stuck in the ice, and someone needed to save your arse." Gisela glared, but slowly she softened into confusion. "Rathar. . . what do you mean about Reliquary?" Rathar's eyes widened. Arguing with Gisela never earned him any laurels. She drew out words from him in contretemps like poison from a wound, and in the end, he walked away the vanquished.

"Damn it, Gisela. I was angry. I didn't mean to say it."

"Well, you said it. What are you not telling me?"

"I don't think now is the best time." Rathar put his hand on Gisela's shoulder, but she shrugged it away.

"Reliquary is my home. You will tell me, and you will tell me forthright." Gisela's voice was commanding, and Rathar felt powerless in all his usual strength. He closed his eyes and honed his senses, checking for anyone that could be listening. When he was satisfied that they were well enough alone, Rathar related to Gisela all that Vivica had told him about the Consortium, the division, the divvying of the northwestern province, and at long last about the handing over of Reliquary to Orien. Gisela felt a burning in her eyes. "What will he do? What will he do to my home?"

"I don't think anything hasty or drastic. Not yet anyway." Rathar exhaled. "Remember he is just a magician, he does not own the Great City, he merely is its benefactor."

"But his power and influence are vast. Who knows what he is capable of, what his intentions are!"

"I don't know, Gisela." Rathar touched her shoulder, and this time she let it remain.

"Rath, you can't go! You can't walk into Reliquary. I. . . I have to go alone."

"I've been told," he growled deep from within. "But I can't leave you alone."

"What? Why not?"

"Gisela! You shifted! What in all the Provinces are we supposed to do about that?"

"Maybe that's a good thing?" she suggested weakly.

"You don't know how to handle that. You got lucky fighting that Notos. Who's to say you can even do it again?" Rathar was getting agitated.

"I don't know." Gisela's voice was growing fainter, and Rathar felt for a moment that maybe he was being too hard on her.

"Listen. You and I, we are a team. We are going to figure this out together as we do in all matters, and nothing bad is going to happen to Reliquary; I'll make sure of it."

"Rath, you fight aspirmeygs, not magicians."

"You said it before, times are changing. I have a feeling we're all going to have to do our fair share of fighting." Rathar sighed. "Come. Let's go watch a blasted assassin sleep in my Temple." Gisela smiled. When they walked into the Temple, Quilla had head down and her hands folded in a devotional posture.

"Just saying my prayers before bed!" She winked. Gisela glanced with a smirk up at Rathar.

"I'm still not sleeping," he huffed.

$$\bullet\bullet \text{———} \bullet\bullet\bullet\bullet\bullet \text{———} \bullet\bullet$$

Morning came with no incident. Quilla slept soundly, Gisela less so on account of Quilla's deafening, drunk snoring, and Rathar had stayed up all night to watch nothing. Feeling slightly hangdog over the entire affair, Rathar left them to their breakfast at the Temple and ventured out into the streets. His mission was aimless physically, but he intended to clear his mind as best he could. He kept to the back alleys, though no one would readily recognize Gisela walking through the markets and the squares, for Rathar to roam freely was much more dangerous. *Though* he thought to himself, *now Gisela might be in danger, too.* He walked slowly, a pace he was unaccustomed to, trailing his fingers carelessly on the buildings that flanked him. He let his mind wander as aimlessly as his steps. He thought about the first day he had arrived at Borghild; it had been sleeting so hard he thought surely the dark clouds themselves would topple out of the sky, and his hands were so cold that when the mistress took them in hers, he thought surely she would cut them off and leave him with two bootless stumps. But instead she breathed a spell of warmth into his bantling body and revived him. He thought about his first kill outside of Borghild; it hadn't even been an aspirmeyg; the Provinces were full of fell beasts besides aspirmeygs and one was bound to happen upon them trekking through the wilds. He thought about his favourite tavern. He thought about his least favourite tavern. He thought about where he'd like to go with Gisela if he could leave all this foul magician nonsense behind him. He thought, but his thoughts were abruptly halted by the sound of struggle coming from a nearing alleyway.

"No, no. I rather think you don't want to do that, sirs," came a stuttering echo from the alley just barely draped in sunlight.

"Empty your pockets, little man, or we strew your guts upon the ground," a gruff voice answered in turn.

"Yes, yes, I was afraid of that, quite so. Nasty business, robbing people."

Rathar tilted his ear toward the voice; it was familiar. He sprinted toward it. "Wells!"

"My, my, if that isn't you, Stalker! You'd best get out of here before you find yourself in a nasty bind." Wells smiled despite his unfortunate situation.

"I don't mean to offend you," Rathar said, "but I don't think I'm the one in a bind." He drew his blade at the large man towering over Wells's scrawny, gaunt figure that even his tunic couldn't add the appearance of meat to.

"No need, Stalker, no need for bloodshed here, no, no," said Wells, shaking his head.

"We'll see about that," grumbled the man in the alley. Wells pulled an Azaelea flower from his pocket and trailed along the petals with his fingers mumbling something under his breath; suddenly he extended his arm before him and in a flash of crimson light the large man dropped to his knees and began to vomit violently. He clutched at his stomach, grimacing and rolled on the cold stones and filth of the alley. "Oh, dear Stalker do not be alarmed, no, no, you see, magic is all in potential, and I have merely drawn the potential from the toxin of this rhododendron and exerted it hither. He will collect himself in time, but let us not linger, hmm?"

"You're a. . ."

"A magician. Yes, yes. Well, an ex-magician, rather. I believe the term is *going rouge*. You see, me specialty is toxins and poisons being an herbalist, and that's considered black magic by the Consortium." Wells smiled sheepishly. "I've always preferred the art of the apothecary to flashing lights, anyway. Something about mixing things, yes, mixing with your hands, you know?" Rathar looked at the bony shadow of a man before him with his mouth slightly hanging open.

"Stalker, tell me," said Wells pulling Rathar along by the arm, in a jolly mood for someone who had just been threatened by a man twice his size, "how did that henbane work out, yes yes, how did it take?"

"Uh, it took." Rathar struggled to spit out the words, still looking over his shoulder at the man frozen on the ground. "Wells, what are you doing in Adonica?" He finally turned his attention to his companion as they weaved through the alleys, clearly with a destination in mind.

"You see, Stalker, I—"

"Rathar."

"Right, yes, yes, of course. Rathar. Strong name for a strong lad!" Wells laughed, patting Rathar on the arm. "My apothecary was burned. Right to the ground. That whole to-do in Lanthchilde where they burned that Stalker and Vestal at the stake you know. Terrible thing they did. The burning I mean. I have a hard time believing those people were truly murderers. I rather like your kind! Keep my kind alive." Wells laughed again and halted in front of a pile of bricks. One by one he carefully began to remove them. "This is all I have left, Stalker. Yes, yes, what little I could make out with, enough to help who I could along the road if need be." Slowly, as he laid aside the bricks, there was revealed a fair wooden box with a chestnut handle on the top; the front presented two wooden doors shut with a few leather straps and brass buckles. It looked heavy, but Wells lifted it with no trouble at all.

"That's what's left of the apothecary?" Rathar raised his brows. "So why here?"

"Well I hid it here so nobody would steal—"

"No, why here? Adonica."

"Ah, yes, yes, well you see, the Adonican Valley is just beyond this city, I can find there more herbs, more ingredients. I intend to rebuild. The only trouble is that the wild places are crawling with aspirmeygs they say, more than ever is the rumour."

"Is that the rumour?" Rathar squinted.

"I say, Stalker, are you holed up in a whorehouse without a shred of news? All winter gathering west across the Adonican Valley, aspirmeygs have been seen in untold numbers. Your kind are in high demand!" Wells chuckled and heaved his box over his shoulder. "I'd better get going, Rathar." He enunciated obnoxiously, or Rathar thought so.

"Wait." Rathar reached his hand out. "I have a proposition, rogue. Come with me."

"Oh! I bring home an assassin, but *you* bring home a *magician*?! Does your memory not serve you? We have a fair few of those out to kill us, Rathar!" Gisela's hands were on her hips in a defiant pose as the two stood in the Temple doorway, Rathar trying to explain their newest addition.

"You know, it's really not ladylike to argue."

"A rogue you say! Then he doesn't even claim a faction! A side of the division!"

"I don't know if he even knows about the division. Look at him. . . if this fellow chose sides, he'd have resources, and if he had resources. . . he'd be. . . fatter."

"Rathar, this is not a joke!"

"And I'm no jester." Rathar inhaled sharply and looked directly into Gisela's piercing, grey eyes. "We need a magician to figure out why you shifted. I found one. You need a companion to help you get to Reliquary alive. I think you found that, too." They both turned and looked into the Temple. It was a sight; Quilla, sprawled out on the glazed tile floor telling tales with raucous laughter of gruesome hits and close encounters, as Wells related to her the many satisfactions that herbs held over magic, showing off the delights of his ligneous chest. Both unexpected encounters, surely, but perhaps, thought Rathar, a sort of providence, if such a thing even existed.

"God is with us." Gisela sighed, sounding more like she was trying to convince herself than anyone else.

Chapter

08

V IVICA REMOVED HER HANDS FROM the crystal ball and let it fall into darkness, leaning back into her wicker chair. Her eyes closed and her brow furrowed in deep concern. The Consortium had divided; the fractures had surely reached further than the northwestern province. Orien persuaded members of influence to divide for a reason that was unknown, but something large was afoot. Reliquary was in the hands of what she could only now describe as an enemy, and they would have to tread lightly, and gather intelligence. Vivica knew who she couldn't trust, but who she could trust was an entirely different affair. Luanda, surely, was as good a friend as any, still, but what of Favian? What of Rose? They may have been on her side of the Consortium's division, but that meant nothing in the current moment. Vivica sighed and gently pulled a lilac, velvet cloth from a cluster of crystal balls all filled with the images of various Stalkers. Though she couldn't contact them through these, she could watch them, keep an eye on them, each and every one that she had reared. The Stalkers came from a completely isolated population hidden in the mountains of Rotrude; it was a hearty culture, a culture that lived to reproduce the most ideal specimens and left the weakest and defective children exposed on the mountaintops to die. One had developed a persistent respiratory illness, another simply the wrong colour of eyes, another was knock-kneed. These children, though not ideal to their own race, were of course much more capable than any man, dwarf, elf, or magician throughout the Provinces in their physical abilities. When the first Stalkers of the Provinces came down from the Mountains of Rotrude to help deter the rising threat of the aspirmeygs, they were the only race aspirmeygs had proven corporeal against, but they soon scuffled with the magicians of old and retreated back to their mountain isolation, offering up as an insult their discarded offspring. Vivica created the keep of Borghild where she took in every exposed child and raised him, in the same harshness of their combative culture, raised him for war with the aspirmeygs, for a life on the road, but all the same with the tenderness of a mother, calling them Stalkers as legend called their native race before they took on the disaffectionate designation, wights; however after a tragic accident it was devised that they would be matched with a Vestal and sent out to preserve the races of the world in exchange for life and silver. She loved each one, though she did not expect the same in return. Though they could be polite enough to walk through a town without causing disaster, Stalkers were an obstreperous and uncouth people, quite simply devoid of love down to their genetics. "Still," Vivica said aloud to herself, "there is not a thing I wouldn't do for those boys." She sighed and leaned back into her chair again, tossing the velvet piece onto the floor beside her. She needed a plan. She needed rest. "Rest comes after the task," she mumbled. That is what she always taught the boys. The job comes first. Vivica stood and aligned her shoulders proudly. Then she held her palm upwards, breathed warmth into it, igniting first a spark and then a brilliant amethyst flame. "Brangian." She spoke clearly, and the flame consumed her, transporting her at once in a fiery portal from where she stood to her intended.

•• ———— ••●•• ———— ••

"We can't just wait around for Vivica. We're sitting ducks," explained Rathar. Though he had a deep respect for the wishes of his mistress, he had always been of his own mind, ready to act on his own instincts, and with danger looming, the thought of hanging fire gave him a sour stomach.

"You bet I'm in! Whose soft belly shall I run through? Whose ugly neck should be adorned by my garrote?" Quilla jumped to her feet and swung the rapier from her waist through the air with a sharp, whining sound that made Wells jerk nervously.

"Anyone who gets in her way." Rathar gestured to Gisela.

"Rath!" Gisela winced.

"I mean it. I need Gisela in and out of Reliquary safely. Are you the woman for the job?" Rathar looked intently at Quilla, and for a moment her playfulness vanished. She resheathed her blade and sat lazy-legged before him.

"I'm a professional, sir. I'll get your lady wherever you want her without a scratch on her. As for the other fellows. . . my face will be the last thing they remember." And suddenly she stuck out her tongue and crossed her eyes with a roar of laughter.

"I trust her, Rathar. I'm not afraid." Gisela smiled softly.

"I want her there and *back to me* then. Without a scratch on her. As for you," Rathar turned toward Wells, "I need a favour, and to repay you I'm going make sure you don't die while you're... picking flowers for your... box."

"Why, my my, Stalker, you mean it, do you?"

"Well, you say there's an aspirmeyg dilemma. That's my occupation."

"Yes, yes, that would be wonderful, just wonderful! What is it that you'll be needing then, Rathar? Some more henbane? Hmmm? Some roots?" Wells inquired gleefully.

"I need a magician." Rathar frowned and in a hushed and bridled voice, he recounted the story of the Notos and how Gisela had shifted and slew it by her own might.

"There is a link between you and Gisela here. Hmmm, my, my, you shared your power with her somehow." Wells rubbed the bridge of his nose under his glasses between thumb and finger.

"What?" Rathar and Gisela both asked eagerly.

"Vestals give, you see, that is their power. They do not take. So what power she received was a gift, yes, yes."

"Go on," Rathar urged.

"I intend to earn my bodyguard, yes, yes." Wells smiled. "Well, both of you sit back-to-back, won't you? With your heads touching yes, my, my I'd like to discern what is being shared here." Rathar and Gisela did as they were told, sitting back-to-back with their heads touching, though the top of Gisela's head only nearly reached the bottom of Rathar's. "Might tickle!" Wells chuckled, "or. . . burn. . . or my, my, you might go blind, haven't given the old magic a go in quite some time." Rathar's frame tensed up like timber seized by frost. Gisela remained calm and only squeezed his hand reassuringly.

"That would be fantastic!" Quilla chimed in, almost bouncing up and down. Wells placed a hand on both Gisela's and Rathar's heads and began to recite an incantation in a low a rumbling voice that sounded as though it could not possibly come from the likes of his scrawny, hollow body, and for a moment Rathar felt as if he did go blind for there was a flash so bright that everything went black for a time, black and silent as death, or at least he thought he must be dead because there was nothing all around him. Nothing to see, nothing to hear, until he heard a faint familiar voice calling his name.

"Rathar? Rath. . . are you okay? Rath?" It was Gisela, her voice was bright like a song that pierced the nothingness around him. The tone was that of a mother but almost of a child all in one; he wanted to stay in the darkness and listen, to just stay and listen, but suddenly he opened his eyes and gasped for air as if he'd been drowning. "Rathar! By God, breathe!" Gisela pulled him by his arm into a sitting position, he'd been lying on the floor for how long he didn't know. Rathar looked around him. Gisela was kneeling beside him looking very concerned, Quilla was standing over Gisela looking intrigued and rather amused, and Wells stood running his hands through his messy, ashen hair looking downright confused.

"My, my." Wells stuttered.

"We aren't blind." Rathar rubbed his temples and looked up at Wells for answers, "But let's not do that again."

"Get to the good stuff, herb man! How did the big guy share his power?" Quilla patted her knees eagerly.

"Love," Wells whispered.

"Listen, he's no dog, but he ain't no puppy either!" Quilla burst into laughter.

"Wells," Gisela said with as much tact and gentleness as she could manage, "Stalkers, they aren't, well it's not that Rathar isn't kindly. . . he's. . . but. . ."

"Stalkers don't love. Do it again," Rathar growled ferociously, causing even Quilla to silence herself.

"There is no need, Rathar." Wells adjusted the spectacles on his nose. "No, no need. I have performed the reading rune correctly. You are capable of love. It is why the Vestal does not influence you; love for the common man keeps you from murder, see that is altogether a different kind of love, there are many types of love which rule the heart. Yes, yes, it is why you were able to transmit your power into a vessel of trust during a moment of need. The only question, Stalker, is who do you love so potently that you were able to transfer *such power*? For I fear, yes, yes, I fear that if something happens to this person you are capable also of great hatred. My, my you are powerful."

"Who I love?" Rathar said, almost in disbelief.

"Isn't it obvious?" whispered Gisela. She placed a hand softly on his shoulder. "You love Vivica. She raised you like a mother, when all you have left of your own is a fading image of a woman who left you behind to die."

"I suppose. . . I do," Rathar mumbled.

"And you needn't worry of a thing happening to her, what with her power and her security at Borghild." Gisela smiled.

"Wells. . . but I gave my power to Gisela. . ." Rathar was still trying to fit the pieces together like an intricate puzzle.

"As a Stalker with control over yourself, you have control of your gifts. Apparently, that means transferring them to a vessel of your choosing." Rathar stared at him incredulously.

"I can do it again?"

"I don't see why not, no, no, I certainly don't." Wells grinned. Rathar turned to Gisela and looked at her with hesitation.

"There are a lot of aspirmeygs from here to Reliquary," he grunted.

"I want some!" Quilla shrieked, and in unison her other three companions responded with a resounding "No!"

●● ———— ●●●●● ———— ●●

The sun had not yet risen when Rathar shook Gisela awake beneath her cloak. Twigs snapped and leaves rustled beneath her as she rolled over. With new travelling companions, they were no longer welcome to stay in the Temples reserved for Stalkers and Vestals alone, so they had made their camp in the woods outside Adonica.

"It's not yet morning," Gisela whispered, not ready to wake Quilla and face her enthusiasm so early.

"I know. I want to speak with you." Gisela sighed lightly and got up, wrapping her cloak tightly around her shoulders; spring had not yet shaken off the chill of its nascence. "Listen carefully to me, and do not give me your answer until you have considered my thoughts," Rathar whispered as they walked. "Forget Wells, forget

Quilla, forget going west. I'll come with you to Reliquary. It'll be safer that way. Nobody can protect you the way I can, the way I have for years, Sela." Gisela paused for a moment to feign being in thought. She did not want Rathar to think that his convictions were invaluable to her, because in truth she would prefer his company and protection to far-flung ends of the Provinces, but it was not meant to be; they both knew this.

"'Twould be safer for me, but that's a death sentence for you, Rath. Orien is waiting for you to head that direction. And—"

"Sela."

"And," she said firmly, "you gave your word to Wells. Besides, you should be taking care of these aspirmeygs."

"And the aspirmeygs between here and Reliquary?" Rathar pushed.

"You aren't the only Stalker out there. Besides. . . you're going to share your power with me."

"As self-defense! Not to hunt!" he instructed; in fact he almost pleaded.

"I know," Gisela said in a soothing and apologetic way. "I know. But we cannot cheat this. We cannot cheat God's way. Reliquary is a necessity, Rathar. Your burdens are heavy. . ." He scoffed and kicked his boots in the dirt. "So, how did you do it? Before. How did you give me your power?"

"I just. . . really hoped you wouldn't die. I couldn't bear to have failed you." Gisela turned to look at Rathar, but his face was down. He was ashamed and would not let his hazel eyes be met. In all their years of slaying beasts together, there had undoubtedly been some close calls, but Rathar always had managed to fight his way out of it, to somehow gain back ground, to find the upper hand once more. This time was different. If not for Gisela, he would have been a corse on the road, and she would have been making her way back to Reliquary, a relict like many of her sisters before. Something had welled up inside of her and urged her to put her sword to the beast knowing full well that success was outside the realm of possibility. Was it God? What stirred inside her so? They walked back to camp together and saw that Quilla and Wells were up and jovial as ever. As far as travelling companions went, they had chosen a merry bunch, especially with the looming threat of death on their tails. "Have you eaten?" Rathar grumbled, picking up his bronze blade from the ground and securing it around his waist. "It's time to practice." Together the four headed through the woods.

"Halt here, yes, yes," commanded Wells in a stammer. "Now, usually you would hone your senses of course, but perhaps Gisela should seek out the, prey, we might call it."

"How?" Rathar rasped, "She's in no danger now. Anyway, I had shifted first."

"Correct, Stalker, but I think, yes, I think if you focus on that which you love, it will come more easily." Rathar moved about from foot to foot uncomfortably.

"Fine," he grunted. He closed his eyes and tried to focus on Vivica. He remembered what was obvious at first. That she smelled of evergreen, her dark lips twisted up into a mischievous smile, her long hair brushing up against his face as a child when she had leaned over him dreadfully sick in bed or healing a broken bone. What power it took to break the bone of a Stalker. He remembered that in the harsh world of growing up to kill aspirmeygs, she had provided a home where even laughter could exist, because he had been only a child after all. Yes, she had been the mother he never had, and surely he loved her for it. That his brothers could not seemed in a trice unfathomable, contemptible even; but Rathar knew the nature of wights, and could not hold this contempt within himself for more than a fleeting moment. The respect that Stalkers held for their mistress was fondness enough. "Now," said Wells, "yes, yes, now that you are in control of yourself, transfer your power." Rathar squinted his eyes together, sweat gathering on his brow and tried with all his might to turn over his power to Gisela. When he opened his eyes, he was amazed at what stood before him. On Gisela's fair skin were faint traces of crimson from her wrists to her elbows. She was turning her arms over, admiring them, but just as soon as they appeared, they vanished.

"It worked!" Quilla squealed.

"Hardly." Rathar was quick to squash her enthusiasm.

"She couldn't detect an aspirmeyg that way, much less a damned squirrel."

"You are new to the revelation of love, Stalker, yes, yes, it will take time, but soon we will have it." Wells grinned from ear to ear. Days passed, however, and though Rathar tried time and time again to focus on his love, there was never more than a faint glow skimming Gisela's body; he could never reproduce the shifting Gisela needed for safe passage to Reliquary.

"Rath?" Gisela tiptoed over to the edge of a small brook where Rathar sat, brooding. "We need to speak," she said quietly. Rathar said nothing in reply and only looked forward into the bubbling water as Gisela sat beside him. She breathed a heavy sigh before resting her head on her companion's shoulder. "Listen, there are a fair few Stalkers out there to mind the wilds and the roads, and I suppose at this point. . . I suppose we're wasting time. I have to go to Reliquary. No more beating around the bush, Rath. No more 'sitting ducks.' It's time to go. And you listen to me, I'm not afraid. I've learned countless things by your side these many years, and one has been to extinguish my fear, just as a Stalker, so courageous in the face of many dangers."

"I do not feel courageous." Rathar breathed. "I fear to let you but a league out of my sight."

"I will be capable without you, Rathar. You shall see when I return."

"What of I without you?"

Gisela reached into the folds of her brown, Vestal's robes and pulled out a small, white bouquet. "Lily of the Valley. I guess it's sort of cheating; I didn't pick them. I stole them from Well's chest, but. . . before I go, does it please you?" Gisela smiled warmly and held out the handful of flowers to Rathar. His heart sank to his stomach. Lily of the Valley was an omen of death; he'd learned that from Vivica when he was a boy. For a moment he looked into her glittering grey eyes and said nothing. He didn't know what to say; he had felt many times the effects of many wounds both insignificant and severe, but in this moment, he felt as if he were literally dying, as if something were attacking him from the inside of his chest, like some sort of beast or terrible injury, but then. . . warmth, everything faded into warmth.

"Take it. It's yours," he mumbled in disbelief.

"What?" Gisela reached for her eyes as her vision went black as night. She could feel the growth of something, something like vines covering her eyelids and her blood was racing through her body; she breathed in through her nose and suddenly she no longer missed her vision anymore, for her smell laid out a map for her that her eyes never could. "Rathar?"

Rathar touched her arm, pulsing with the unmistakable contusions of a Stalker. She had shifted in full. "Can you help yourself shift back?"

Gisela carefully placed her own thumbs on her eyelids and released the influence of overwhelming calm that helped Rathar shift back so often, and slowly but surely the sinews and flickering, wound-like patches of the Stalker's power left her.

"I'll have to get used to that." She swayed and fell onto one knee; the pain of shifting back was overwhelming. "Rath! You did it! You must have remembered something from your childhood about Vivica that was quite strong!" Gisela reached down and picking up the flowers she had dropped, she tucked them into Rathar's hand, trying not to lose her balance.

"Damn," he said, wide-eyed, shaking his head and helped her stagger back to camp.

•• ———— ••●•• ———— ••

"You feel as though you can call on it at any time now?" Wells adjusted his spectacles in astonishment.

"Yes. He truly shared it with me! You should have seen it!" Gisela exclaimed but then winced in pain; she hadn't yet recovered from shifting back and was leaning heavily against a tree stump.

"We'll be unstoppable now! You and me! Kicking arses from here to Reliquary!" Quilla giggled like a little girl.

"You're quiet, Rathar, yes, yes, you must be pleased." Wells raised his brow.

"Pleased," Rathar mumbled quietly, as if to himself. "I'm pleased."

"That's it then. We split tomorrow morning." Gisela adjusted herself with a slight grimace. "Quilla and I will go north to Reliquary. Wells and Rathar will go west to deal with the aspirmeygs."

"You two take the horses." Rathar gestured to Gisela and Quilla. "Your errand requires haste, and they make a speedier getaway." Nobody slept long that night, even Rathar preferred to stay up enjoying the company for the last while. Quilla told dirty jokes that made Wells and Gisela blush. Rathar was persuaded to tell a few tall tales about his most daring adventures, and Gisela sang songs all to the amusement of everyone. But it did not last, and morning came swifter than anyone would have liked. The camp was somber as the sun rose. When finally everything was packed up, and all traces of their whereabouts had been taken up, Quilla and Gisela mounted their horses and turned north. "Don't do anything to draw attention to yourselves."

"Don't worry, Rath, we won't."

"And Sela. . ."

"You don't have to say anything further." She smiled.

"I would. . . I would hate if something happened to you." He chose his words carefully and then smacked Leif on the rear urging the horses onwards as Gisela looked back bemused.

"You may never see her again, Stalker." Wells crossed his skinny arms and watched the horses ride away.

"A lot of people are going to die if I never see her again, magician," Rathar growled savagely, and for a moment, as everything "different" about him melted away, Wells saw in him the uncontrollable monster he had the potential to be. "Let's move." Rathar swung his pack over his shoulder, and they headed west.

Chapter

09

"**V**IVICA!" LUANDA COULDN'T CONCEAL HER surprise as Vivica's figure burst forth from amethyst flames; she urged the footmen from the room, shutting the towering cedar doors behind them and dusted her slender hands on a samite dress that was hemmed just below the knee. "Showing up in places that are no longer too friendly..." Luanda's eyes darted to where the footmen had receded and she reached her hand in front of her and made a fist, instantly drawing shut the satiny drapes that lined the tall windows surrounding the circular tower, "it isn't the wisest of moves."

"Moves must be made, my dear. It is time."

"What moves, I inquire? We are manipulators, not readers of prophecies. We know nothing until that scrappy Vestal and her Stalker protector get to Reliquary. Then can moves be made perhaps, if anything even comes of this prophecy."

"Luanda, you know, you feel it deep within you, something very dark is behind the splitting of the Consortium. It is not simply politics."

"Yes." Luanda's face settled into a pretty pout. "Aspirmeygs, Vivica, the northwest is crawling with them. I don't know what, but there is something fell in the air lately."

"We need Reliquary, but Rathar and Gisela need a magician. If I start working within spitting distance of the north, Orien and the rest will grow suspect. No, I need you, Luanda, to go to them. You've been reassigned to Isolde and to reach there. . . you could travel through Adonica."

"Of course; I see." Luanda nodded earnestly, resting her pretty chin on her fingers. "But, Vivica, how is it that you dare to come as far north as Brangian? I'm more than halfway to Reliquary from Adonica!" Luanda's pixie-like features were best expressed in surprise.

"Haven't you heard, darling? I'm dead. They have falsified my corse for the cause." Vivica's face was somber. "My errand is for my *family*, but I'd best not linger."

"What am I to do when I find them, Rathar and Gisela?"

"Rathar will tell you everything. I think it's better that you know little for now. It will bring you less risk if you're encountered. But know this, it is a most unnatural situation and requires a talented and trusted hand. That is why I have come to you, my dear."

"I understand," Luanda said sternly. "I'll leave just as soon as I can. You must understand if I go on foot and cloaked to avoid any detection or an escort; the duke of Brangian will notice if any of his prized horses are missing for any length. But where will you go?"

"There is something I must look into in Gundrada. And Luanda, my darling, the footmen. Deal with them. Choke them with their own tongues if you have to. I can't have any eyes on me here." Vivica smiled and summoned back into her palm the portal of amethyst flame, intending next to proceed toward Gundrada.

Chapter

10

"WE GET SO MUCH FARTHER on horses than on foot," Quilla chirruped happily, but Gisela seemed preoccupied or in a dream; her fingers danced back and forth over the reins wearing her thoughts into the strap. "I had a horse, before I came to Adonica that is," she continued, "but the poor beast was worse for wear, and so was I really, so I had to eat him. Roasted him right over the fire." Quilla looked back at Gisela trotting along beside her. "First, I skinned him and made a jacket, but it wasn't very warm. . . because, you know, thin skinned, useless beast. . . it was a horse!" she cupped her hands around her mouth and shouted the last bit.

"What's that?" Gisela looked up. Quilla was a very different sort of company than Rathar, louder certainly and more of a constant source of noise, but Gisela had been entirely distracted.

"I all but threatened to roast Leif over the fire, and you all but handed him over, that's what," Quilla scoffed.

"I'm sorry it's just. . . something Rath said, it has me thinking."

"Woof woof?"

"Very funny, Quilla."

"I've been thinking, you should call me Quill. You know, now that we're friends. That's what you and Rathar do anyhow." Quilla grinned wide, and Gisela couldn't help but smile back.

"Then you'll call me Sela. Now that we're friends."

"Sela and Quill, horse-killers, beast-hunters, sneaks, and prophets!"

"That's a bit. . . extravagant," Gisela laughed and blushed slightly. "I'm only a Vestal." They rode on in nothing close to silence for a long while until Quilla called out,

"Look! There's a town up ahead."

Gisela trotted up beside her and nodded. "Yes, that's Jabr. A dwarven village. It has a small Temple, so I should be able to get some silver for the road. They aren't the friendliest of sorts, but if you keep to yourself—"

"You, Sela, just don't know how to *be a dwarf*," Quilla reeled with laughter. As they approached the Temple past the main gate of Jabr, a rather stern looking dwarf stood in front of the door as Gisela dismounted Leif.

"Good afternoon, would you be the ledger-man?"

"You'll be getting shite if you expect the ledger-man." The dwarf leaned forward and spat on the ground.

"Sir, I'm a Vestal. I'm only here to take what is owed to me."

"Yer a Vestal alright, without a Stalker. No Stalker means no work. No work means no feckin' money." The dwarf crossed his arms over his chest and smirked as Gisela mounted Leif frowning.

"Hey, shite-for-brains," Quilla called out from atop her own horse. "Where's the feckin' ale round here?"

The dwarf cracked a smile and pointed around the corner of the long street.

"What are you doing?" Gisela tugged on Quilla's tunic.

"Taking what we're owed." She smiled deviously. The ceilings in the tavern were so low that Gisela and Quilla had to crouch slightly, but Quilla made a grand entrance. She kicked open the door with her heavy boots and within five minutes of sitting down at a dimly lit table in the back, loudly announced to the room that she could outwit any dwarf in the room with a game of cards. She also made sure to stomp her feet, add in a few curse words, and spit on the floor. Gisela was horrified, and the dwarves went wild. Gisela had never been anywhere in Jabr outside of the Temple, as per Rathar's rules in that he didn't have much patience for dwarves, and she was entirely out of her element; the raucousness was deafening, and the smell certainly left something to be desired; the very walls reeked of piss, marrow, and alcohol as Quilla had not so delicately stated upon their arrival. Quilla, however, seemed to be right at home in the dimly lit hovel.

"Give me the purse," Quilla whispered.

"I thought you were *making* money."

"You've got to spend money to make money," Quilla quipped and then shouted, "Free ale for anyone who will play me! Two ales! Triples!" Gisela watched as coin after coin left her purse and dwarf after dwarf sat drunk at the table playing Quilla in some confounded card game, but as the afternoon lingered on into evening, Gisela noticed that the purse started filling back up, and the rules of the game became more and more convoluted.

"That wasn't a damned rule five minutes ago," hiccoughed a dwarf with a beard as yellow as straw that bristled up against a round, red nose that Gisela thought looked remarkably like a tomato.

"It was so, you just weren't paying attention!" Quilla slapped down three cards in an accusatory fashion. "Now, draw two because you lost that round for. . . uh. . . yelling. In the rules, I clearly stated you couldn't yell at the dealer. Penalty."

The yellow-bearded dwarf cursed and all surrounding him lamented his situation, but drank to it with whooping laughter.

"Well, gentlemen, you all lose, and it's getting late. Maybe we'll play again sometime!" Quilla scooped up the remaining silver coins from the table and stuffed them into the now full leather purse. "Ninny tipplers, the lot of them." She winked at Gisela. The dwarves all shouted in general rowdiness and discontent as the pair made their way to the door to go, but as Quilla prepared for an equally spectacular exit, the ledger-man from the Temple ran in, out of breath and white as a sheet.

"Find a Stalker, somebody! There's an aspirmeyg!"

"You feckin' old coot," the tomato-nosed dwarf roared, didn't you check the Temple?"

"Temple's empty! It's in the square!" The ledger-man cried and then ran for the back of the tavern, hiding himself beneath a table. Gisela and Quilla looked at each other and both pushed their way through the sea of drunken dwarves out of the tavern, spilling a few silver coins onto the floor along the way.

"We have to find it!" Gisela shouted.

"Sela. . . Rathar said not to do anything to draw attention to ourselves. What we have to do is *leave*."

"There's an aspirmeyg *in the village*! People are going to die if we don't help." Gisela took Quilla by the hand. "Quill, please."

"Alright, but don't tell the puppy I said okay! This is absolutely on you!" They took off running toward the village square. *I can do this*, Gisela thought to herself. *If he can do it, I can do it. He gave it to me.* Gisela closed her eyes as she was running and allowed her eyes to become impotent and grown over. She inhaled deeply, and soon it was her sense of smell that was creating a survey of her surroundings, intricate and detailed. She could feel every vein twisting up her arms and coiling around her neck pulsing wildly and adding to her strength; she was grateful to her modest Vestal's robes for covering the red, bruise-like markings that were consuming her body lest she frighten anyone.

"I smell it," she said.

"What? Where?" Quilla looked around. They still weren't at the square, but Gisela took off like a shot from Quilla's side. The Eurus soared over Gisela, the height of two strong men, surging around it crashing waves of wisping water. Where it slammed down its might with jagged claws, cloudy pools splashed and filled the square. Gisela watched as dwarves writhed around in the square shrieking in horror as their guts splayed out on the pavement next to them, spilling out of their sliced open bellies, still others drowning in torrents of water that were not even there. She herself waded knee deep in an oncoming rush. Concealed by the chaos of the square, Gisela took the opportunity and lunged at the beast from behind with her bronze sword drawn at her shoulders, plunging at its thigh. The hit was successful, and the

Eurus staggered, looking around in a fury for its enemy. Gisela, however, was swift, and having spun to her left around the beast's side, slashed at its belly. The rapids were mixed with dark purple as the Eurus began to bleed out, but it would not be taken so easily; she did not possess all the strength of Rathar, and her cut was not deep enough.

Gisela braced herself against the torrent and called loudly, "Beast of the shadow water, your rival is here!" And with madness in its foggy eyes, the Eurus turned and rushed downward toward Gisela, but having fixed her position firmly and confidently, she inhaled deeply through her nose; as it leaned forward, she plunged her blade up through its chin until it shone through the top of its great, bald head, and the Eurus toppled to the ground, leaving behind a gush of hazy purple. Gisela breathed deeply to settle the rattling breaths that this newness brought her, and she placed her sticky, purple thumbs onto her eyes, focusing on releasing calm. She furrowed her brow in pain and fell to her shaking knees as her sight slowly returned, and the marks of the Stalker's affliction vanished.

"My God!" Quilla cried gleefully as she ran through the square, picking up Gisela's blade from the ground and running over to her. "That was amazing! You should have seen yourself! Or. . . smelled yourself, I guess? Hey, are you okay?" Quilla grabbed Gisela by the arm and helped her to stagger to her feet. "Let's get out of here."

"Too late," Gisela winced. They looked around the square and dwarves stood with their mouths agape and their weapons drawn.

"What is she? A magician?" cried the ledger-man.

"She's no damned Stalker!" cried another dwarf with a riot of hoots and hollers behind him. "It's black magic!"

"She saved our lives." The tomato-nosed dwarf from the tavern walked into the square and drew his own blade. "And any of you want to kill her for that, you feckin' go through me." He spat on the ground for good measure. Gisela was starting to realize that was the way of dwarves. The crowd seemed to settle. "Come on," he hiccoughed, still a bit drunk, "get your arses out of here." They walked hastily to the stable where a group of dwarves were standing with their weapons drawn. "Don't worry about them. They're my men. We're the company that looks after the roads round south. We're in debt to you, Vestal." He hiccoughed again. "Name's Kaleb. You need anything, you know where to find us." Kaleb handed Gisela the reins of Leif and the unnamed horse. "But I wouldn't keep going around and doing shite so. . . unnatural." He twisted up his face.

"Thank you, Kaleb." Gisela struggled onto her horse, and sighed, relieved to have somewhere to sit. "God is with you." She nodded, and they left Jabr in the dark.

•• ———— ••●•• ———— ••

After they had ridden all of the day and into the night, Quilla could no longer stifle her yawning.

"Hone those senses and find us a safe place to camp. It's late, and I'm beat!" Then she twiddled her thumbs embarrassed, "Well I mean. . . you did all the hard work. . . but I did get the silver, and that's all mental, you know? So mentally. . . I'm aweary." Gisela smiled slightly, but she agreed. She was completely exhausted and in pain from shifting. She had a newfound appreciation for Rathar and the physical burden he sustained day in and day out; his strength had always seemed so unwavering that it gave nothing away, hardly an ache or a throb. She closed her eyes and focused on her senses. Hearing. Smelling. Even opening her mouth to taste the air. There was neither a body nor a creature anywhere near.

"Here is good," Gisela sighed and pulled Leif off the road and into the murky woods. When they had tied up the horses and laid out their cloaks, Gisela and Quilla relaxed by a crackling fire. Quilla counted the silver coins she had made, glinting in the glow of the flame, and Gisela closed her eyes and tried to ease what parts of her body were still smarting.

"These powers are certainly something, but I tell you, I was not made with the body to exploit them. What I'd give for some draught to ease this soreness," Gisela sighed.

"Tell me something," Quilla said, jingling the bag of coins against her inner thigh. "What did Rathar say that has you in such a brume anyway?"

Gisela stared into the heart of the bramble blaze. "He said. . . he said he would hate it if something happened to me."

"Ah!" Quilla grinned, and her white teeth flashed. "Well, makes sense."

"It would only make sense if—"

"If he loved you? Yeah. Imagine that. The puppy that worries about you all the time and wants to risk his life for you. Yeah, I wonder if he loves you? Vivica my arse." Quilla tossed the coin purse at her bag. "You pick flowers for each other!" She grabbed her belly and laughed.

"But I'm—"

"Apparently, you're pretty special, Sela. To somebody anyway." Quilla looked around pretending to check for eavesdroppers and leaned in close. "Here's the question. Do you love him back?" She scrunched her nose and giggled. As the night went on, the fire died slowly, and Gisela and Quilla welcomed sleep gladly, curled up closely together, as if good friends.

Chapter

11

"YOU LOOK RATHER WORSE FOR wear." Wells smiled, tucking handfuls of roots into the open drawers of his apothecary chest. Rathar had fitted it with straps for his shoulders, and he had been happily carrying it throughout the fields for days picking herbs and digging roots with a small, worn spade. He stood from his knees and waved to Rathar as he stalked in from the field bathed in evening light.

"I killed three aspirmeygs today. I *feel* thus."

"You've been ceaselessly occupied since we entered this valley. I haven't seen you at our camp for, yes yes, two days, Stalker, and the one before that you never set foot in at all!"

"You were right. Aspirmeygs. The land's crawling with them, every kind. Other Stalkers as well. It's all we can do to keep them off the roads for miles in every direction so people can travel."

"Perhaps we'll run into some of your kin!"

"Wouldn't exactly be a happy family reunion." Rathar rolled his eyes and shoved a bloodied few ribs back into place with hardly a hitch in his breath. "I need rest. Shifting back without a Vestal for days on end, it's no easy task."

"Come on then, yes yes." Wells grinned and rummaged through his apothecary chest. "I've foraged something to make a nice, calming brew. Rathar and Wells sat cushioned in the soft spring grass, poking at the fire as the sun sank behind the mountains of Rotrude, a sight growing ever bolder and more explicit as they travelled farther west. Rathar looked at the blood crusted on his knuckles, purple and crimson commingled with ash and soil. He chortled to himself. Gisela would have insisted he wash up, but here, with Wells, they were two filthy men alone in the wild, something he'd always joked with her about preferring, but he didn't prefer it a lick now that she was gone. Perhaps, Rathar thought, when two people grow so accustomed to each other for so long and with such endearment, such attachment, they aren't *meant* to be apart. That had to be the reason for the emptiness he felt inside now, as if his heart was calling out and hearing naught but an echo springing back from his ribs, a cold, cavernous wanting where there once was warmth and fullness.

"Drink up now, Stalker, yes yes, you'll feel revived." Wells handed a steaming clay mug to Rathar that felt coarse against his calloused palms. Rathar sniffed the wafting steam, and the aroma was pleasant enough. "It's better hot, go on, now, go on," Wells urged. Rathar took one long swig from the mug and squeezed his eyes shut hard, trying not to regurgitate the bitter dram. "I don't have very much, no, no, so make sure you swallow that." Wells wagged his finger. Rathar had to force the draught down his throat.

"What sort of dragon piss—" he grimaced and barked, but suddenly every pain in his body began to feel subdued, and he felt almost as if he was floating. "Damn," he murmured and fell back into the grass.

"Potent stuff, yes yes, my own creation. You'll forget those ribs."

"Can't move my. . . ribs. . . Wells? Wells. . . what're you. . . doing?" Rathar mumbled, trying to move his defunct limbs. Wells calmly watched Rathar until he was certain of his total immobility, then he began to tear through Rathar's bags and belongings, turning pockets and pouches inside out, removing his boots, searching relentlessly for what Rathar didn't know, and even if he did, he was helpless as his heavy body succumbed to drooping eyelids.

"W. . . Wells," Rathar slurred, falling into a deep slumber, leaving Wells to his task.

"I'm sorry, Stalker, yes yes, but you see, everyone has chosen a side."

12

"HEY, HEY SELA. WAKE UP already!" Gisela woke up to an uncomfortable rocking on the hard ground. "Wake up!" Quilla shook her again by the shoulders. Gisela opened her eyes and blinked into the sun peeking through the canopy of the forest where they had sheltered off the road. "Gee, I thought you were dead or something." Quilla put her hands on her back and laughed loudly. Gisela groaned at her body; that she lacked the physicality of a Stalker was all too evident to her this morning, sore, feeling every small stone beneath her. "You look pretty rough, Sela, you okay?" Gisela stretched her arms above her head with a crack in both shoulders.

"Don't worry; I'm getting adjusted yet, that's all. It seems I slept too long, though. The sun is up; we should have been on the road hours ago."

"Don't worry! I've been productive!" Quilla held up three, fat-bellied minks by their tails. "I was thinking we could probably make a few satchels for some herbs and tinctures. Rathar used to carry those in his bags, and I think it would come in handy for. . . your new ailments. We should be prepared for anything out here. Also, free meals!"

Gisela smiled widely; she had faith that Quilla would be a good companion, but she had been proving herself to be quite impressive indeed. "That's a great idea; we can stop off at Bethan for some strong thread, and we can gather our tinctures there. Let's gather any useful herbs we see on the way. The only thing is. . . well, it's not that I don't appreciate your hard work. . ."

"Yeah yeah, Vestals don't eat meat, well listen here, you're not a Vestal until we get you to Reliquary. Right now you're a Stalker, and Rathar gave me the task to get you there and back safely. You need to keep up your strength more than ever if you're going to be fighting aspirmeygs or whoever else is out there waiting for you, and if you think you're gonna do that on a belly full of fruits and fungi you're out of your mind, so protein is on the menu, and tonight its name is mink." Quilla nodded assertively and said no more, but smiled to herself taking a small knife from her side and skillfully slicing open the minks, delicately peeling the skins from the meat. The corner of Gisela's mouth turned up slightly, but she sighed audibly. She knew that Quilla was right; what was the point in trying to resist? To eat meat would make her an anomaly to her Vestal sisters, yet here she was, already an anomaly standing in the woods not with her Stalker, who happened to be the man that loved her, but with a stranger who was to be her bodyguard heading to Reliquary for a strange and unknown reason, and fighting aspirmeygs on the way. Gisela's life was an anomaly; eating meat was hardly a ripple on the sea.

Once Quilla had made quick work of the minks, she wrapped the meat in salt and linen to keep the flies away and tucked both it and the skins which she had cleaned most vigorously into her saddle bags.

"Agreed." The two women mounted their horses and set out through the tree cover northward, toward Reliquary where the Scaenus Plains unfurled themselves, on which only a few outposts dotted the land and the Hisanrial made their home.

"Do you think we'll see them? The Hisanrial? They're stuff of legend, you know!" Quilla was standing in the stirrups waving her sword through the air with grand, flourishing movements. Rathar's horse grunted unhappily; it was not yet used to its new, rambunctious master.

"I've been this way many times, to Reliquary and from, but they're very good at not being seen, the Hisanrial. They keep to themselves. The only time I've ever seen one of them is when we hosted one of their messengers at the Abbey."

"You did not!" Quilla spun herself around and sat backwards in the saddle, staring at Gisela with giant eyes, full of wonder. Did he ride his horse bareback, standing on one foot? You know they can do that, don't you?"

"I think that might be a rumour. . . though you might give them a run for their money," Gisela giggled.

"The Hisanrial are master horsemen. They herd the wild horses on the plains and tame them, too; they can do anything! Did you know they can stand on their hands while the horse is cantering, Sela? Did you know that? They're also master trackers;

they can find anything and anyone, anywhere!" Gisela smiled and listened politely to Quilla's made-up tales of the horsemen of the north as they trotted through woods, nearing Bethan.

"And did you know that the Hisanrial are all born bald? It's true! Bald as ass cheeks! They glue horse hair to their heads, but they don't have glue, seeing as they're nomads and all, so they use—"

"Look! That's Bethan up ahead!" Sela chirruped. "Maybe we will have better luck with this Temple; I know the ledger-man here, well." Gisela and Quilla trotted slowly into Bethan; it was charming and friendly; many of the villagers bowed politely seeing Gisela's Vestal's robes. She nodded back in kind, practically singing, "Peace to you." The two trotted past the fountain, where women were gathering water in buckets and laundering a variety of clothes, up the planked main road, lined neatly with stuccoed houses painted in cheerful colours, until the Temple was in view. Gisela dismounted Lief, tied him securely to the hitching post outside the Temple and urged Quilla to follow her.

"Miss Gisela!" A grey-haired and whiskered man leaning on a cane did his best to bow as Gisela and Quilla approached the Temple.

"Quilla, this is Arlen! Arlen has been the ledger-man at the Bethan Temple for. . . well, for as long as I can remember." Gisela smiled warmly.

"It would mean such a great thing," Arlen removed the worn flat cap from his head and clutched it to his breast, "if you would bless me and bless my family, Miss Gisela."

"Of course," Gisela placed one hand gently on Arlen's hands knotted together, and another on his head and she chanted what sounded to Quilla like the most beautiful music she'd ever heard though there was no song. "Peace to you Arlen. Tell me, though I do not have Rathar with me today, may I take at least half of what we are owed from the Temple? We were unfortunately separated today. . ."

"Of course, Miss, of course, but don't be spreading that around," Arlen whispered. "It's the King's law that a Stalker shan't be separated from his Vestal."

"He is at Borghild," Gisela lied. Arlen smiled and reached into his pocket and pulled out a small key to unlock the lockbox at the ledger-man's post. He reached in and took a fistful of silver coins then counted them into the palms of Gisela's hands. "I'm afraid though, Miss Gisela, I can't let your friend stay here, in the Temple that is, seein' that she's not o' the right. . . kind."

"That's no bother, Arlen, you have showed us much kindness already." Arlen blushed. "We will seek residence at the inn near the smithy. I know it to be comfortable. Thank you again."

"Miss!"

"Yes?" Gisela and Quilla turned back to face Arlen as they strode away.

"Tell Mr. Rathar hello for me when you see him. Right nasty lot, Stalkers are. I know they can't but help it, and we are grateful to them o' course, but not Rathar. He's decent folk, the both of ye."

"Is this what it's like to be a Vestal?" Quilla jumped up and down with enthusiasm, again provoking a look of disrespect from Rathar's horse. "They treat you like a queen here!"

"They treat me like a representative," Gisela corrected. "And trust me, it's highly unusual these days."

"What do you mean a representative? Of whom?" Quilla's brows furrowed. Gisela motioned with her head for the pair to turn left onto a narrower path; they now led their horses behind them.

"Of God," Gisela said solemnly. "When I enter a room, when I speak, when I make judgements and act, I am a representative of God." Quilla nodded and scratched her head.

Gisela and Quilla approached the inn at the end of the narrow road, another stuccoed building painted a merry red colour, though Gisela shuddered because it reminded her of the colour of the warm blood that had stained her hands when she had stabbed Merek. They handed their reigns to the stable boy waiting out front and entered. The room was cozy and warm with a large hearth glowing in the middle over which were roasting spits of various meats: legs of venison and lamb and glazed fowl of some different sizes. Men were drying their boots, smoking, and laughing on the left side, eyeing the provocative barmaids on the right who kept pulling items of convenience from their bosoms such as napkins, flint lights, and leather sachets of pipe weed. At the sight of Gisela's entrance, the men sat straight upright and the women scrambled to lace up their blouses.

"Excuse me sir." Gisela and Quilla made their way to the bar at the back of the room. "We need a bed tonight, sir."

"Of course." A huge, brawny man with flaming red hair slapped a wet towel onto the counter and pulled out a worn ledger. "A Vestal without a Stalker, huh?" he grunted, flipping to the end of the ledger. "Why's that?"

"Our separation is our business, sir." Gisela immediately regretted her words.

"Separation." The brawny man scribbled in his ledger. "Well since you're only half a pair, I'll charge you half price, how's that sound?"

"Quite generous sir, but you'll see I do have a companion."

Quilla stepped forward. "Bet I can spit farther than you can." She crossed her arms over her chest and prepared to initiate the challenge.

The man laughed, "We're God-fearing people here. Half price. I like this scrappy one anyway." The man winked as Quilla dropped a few silver coins onto the table.

"What a deal! Thanks, mister!" He bowed at Gisela, letting his gaze linger, picked up the towel and wetted down the counter. "This Vestal stuff has great perks! Let's go gather our herbs and then take a nice, hot bath!" Gisela couldn't argue with that; a hot bath sounded soothing to her aching body and troubled mind.

"I'm not as skilled at herbs as you are," Gisela pursed her lips in thought, "but I could go get the thread and sew our new satchels together; why don't you meet me back here." Quilla nodded and headed toward the apothecary with Gisela's instructions. Bethan was by no means a large village, but it was certainly an intricate system of paths. After a few wrong turns and a few helpful passersby, Quilla found herself in front of a dilapidated stone building with a creaking wooden sign that read in fading blue paint "APOTHECARY." She walked in and the overwhelming scents hit her all at once making her dizzy with chamomile, verbena, basil, rotting roots, vinegar, and violets. She immediately started rummaging through bottles and baskets of herbs, oils, and solutions.

"Hey!" a clear voice came from behind the counter, "Hey I've got those organized!" A handsome young man nimbly hopped over the counter and grabbed Quilla by the wrist.

"Are you going to let go of me, or are you going to lose your hand?" Quilla said feigning sweetness. The young man smiled as he felt the icy cool of steel press against his wrist where it hadn't before.

"Are you going to put down that *expensive* henbane oil?"

"Or what?" Quilla scoffed, but suddenly choked at the feeling of a cold blade on her own neck.

"I must say I am astonished; you pulled that weapon very quickly, but I must insist that you put down the tincture at once. I'd be happy to help you gather what you need. Unless you're here to rob me... in which case, I'm probably going to have to kill you."

Quilla laughed loudly underneath the blade. "What's your name, mister? You're no herb-man; trust me I know what those are like."

"My name is Tycen." Tycen smiled. "This is my friend's shop; I'm here on an errand actually, my supplies have run low, and I need to replenish. He's terribly unorganized, I just thought I'd give him a hand. Tell me, mysterious woman, wielder of the blade, what brings you here?"

"Quilla. The same."

"Hmmm. Vague. Tell me what errand you're here on, Quilla."

"Can't. That's a secret." Quilla smiled and winked. "What about you, oh organizer of bottles?"

"I'm a ranger."

"Say, you any good at these herbs, mister ranger? To tell you the truth, I don't have much of a knack for this sort of thing." Quilla had a sparkle in her eye.

"Quite proficient."

"Well then, Tycen, why don't you help me gather what I need, and then I've got a proposition for you. Say, you got anything for Stalkers?"

•• ———— ••●•• ———— ••

Back at the inn, Gisela sat on the edge of her bed sewing together the sides of the mink skins; they still smelled a bit, but not too badly. They would serve well for the purpose intended. She reached her hand inside of the pouches and stroked the soft fur; it reminded her of Vivica's lovely dresses and the safety of Borghild, but, she thought, the only thing that had made Borghild feel safe for her was Rathar. Gisela had seen other Stalkers and Vestals over the course of her career, and what a chore it looked like to constantly be correcting and influencing the behaviours of beastly men who sought out the pleasures of iniquities; they seemed to have no friendships like she had, only labours. Gisela was either praised for the control she had on Rathar or envied for her lack of work. She knew Rathar was different and how she missed his disparities.

"I've just finished the pouches! You've arrived just in time!" Gisela chirruped as the door to the room creaked open behind her, but when she turned, it was not Quilla standing in the doorway but the brawny red-haired man from behind the bar. Gisela scrambled for her sword laying on her bedside, but the red-haired man was quicker, and he grabbed her arm with his burly hand; there was a muffled *snap*; he pinned it onto her chest and Gisela cried out in pain, but her voice was muted by his other hand over her mouth.

"Can't help you now, can he?" The brawny man chuckled maliciously. "Your precious prayers are worthless, girl." He spat in her face. "You're not going to make it out of this room, and neither your foolish God nor your Stalker can save you now." Gisela's eyes widened in fear. "You'll be dead soon enough. I might as well have some fun." He began to tug at her robes with one hand, freeing her arms, but they were useless to her now, in shock and in pain. Tears welled up in Gisela's eyes, and she shut them and began to pray anyway. At first, she thought it may have been her own tears spilling onto her cheeks, but the hands of the red-haired man stopped moving and she heard a *thud* as his weight lifted off of her. Gisela opened her eyes to Quilla standing above her.

"Gisela! Are you okay?" Quilla was holding a knife dripping in the man's blood—blood that was sprayed all over Gisela. Gisela wiped her eyes with the arm that wasn't aching and sat up. Quilla kicked the corse of the brawny man making sure he was deader than dead.

"Madam," muttered a new voice. "Your arm, I. . . I think it is broken."

Gisela looked down and saw a sharp piece of bone protruding from her flesh. She was still in shock. "We have to leave; we have to leave at once. We have to go back. We have to find Rathar. We have to leave now. Nowhere is safe."

"Sela, calm down. I don't think you're in your right mind just now." Quilla started rummaging through a package, pulling out tinctures. "You can fix that, can't you?"

"Yes," Tycen grimaced, "but fetch me a sedative. She'll not want to be fully awake for this."

13

RATHAR AWOKE FROM A PLEASANT dream of golden curls, but as his eyelids lifted, the dream slowly drifted further and further away from this memory until it was foggy and out of reach. He sat up, and to his surprise, he was leaning against a log at the same camp he'd fallen asleep at; the fire was roaring, his bags were neatly packed next to him, and across from him, at a safe distance, sat Wells, sipping on a clay mug of something hot and steaming.

"Wells!" Rathar stood angrily, swaying for a moment, unsteady on his knees. "What did you do to me? What did you take? What's going on?"

"Now, now, Rathar do be careful, that draught was potent even for a strapping body like yours, yes. Skullcap, valerian, hops, and a bit of elvish calcareous to induce temporary paralysis. It takes quite a bit to bring a body like yours down."

"You said you picked a side, what in all the Provinces does that mean? You explain yourself this moment or I swear your head will be rolling on the ground." Wells shifted back slightly at the savage visage before him and the thought of an angry Stalker bursting right through the flames.

"I don't doubt you, Rathar, I don't doubt you at all, no, no! You see everyone has chosen sides, and you see I had to secure your side."

"I'm on your side! I'm on Gisela's side! I'm sure not on Orien's side! I'm on whoever's side it is that isn't trying to kill me, or drug me for that matter!"

"It's time we had a talk about sides, man to man, yes yes, Rathar." Wells leaned in close. "Go on now, sit, I am terribly afraid you'll fall into the, the fire." Rathar sat down cautiously, but stared daggers at Wells.

"I know about Merek. Well, that is, you see, Merek's imposter. Yes yes." Rathar's mouth dropped open, but nothing came out. He was stunned to silence, and his eyes, previously narrowed, grew wide and slightly alarmed. He took a moment to gather himself and Wells granted it to him.

"Do you have any idea. . . the danger of revealing Borghild to an outsider. . .the. . . the pain that man caused Gisela?" he hissed but almost whimpered at the end. Wells shook his head apologetically.

"Do not fear, it was not I that revealed the secret. You see, when I was in Lanthchilde I was contacted by an acquaintance of mine; you know the name. . . Mirabelle of Dimia."

"Know it enough to know this story isn't going anywhere good," Rathar grunted and stomped his boots in the dirt, preoccupied replaying the image of Gisela's tears and blood-stained frocks over again in his mind.

"She contacted me through a crystal ball, you see, though I do not belong to the Consortium of magicians, they check in on us 'rogues' every once in a while, consider it coercion. You see, that is why, yes, yes, that is why I have had such freedom with my apothecary and—"

"Get to the point, Wells, I know the Consortium is a manipulative, beastly organisation," Rathar growled.

"Right. Yes, yes. She said to me that there was to be a red-haired Stalker, come from Bero to Lanthchilde, and that I was to gather some information for her. Specifically I was to verify that he came that way and determine where he was headed next and verify that he was *alone.*"

"Mirabelle tried to curse Gisela in Bero, and certainly didn't think she'd make it to Lanthchilde. It was thanks to you she lived, Wells. You didn't report this to Mirabelle, did you?"

"But you were alone when I met you; that is what I reported to Mirabelle after all. Now, Rathar, you see, the plot thickens." Rathar breathed a sigh of relief, perhaps they still had the upper hand in a manner of speaking.

"If there's a prophecy in Reliquary, they don't want it read; that's why Mirabelle, in league with Orien, tried to kill Gisela with that seal. So, the burning at the stake of that Stalker and Vestal in Lanthchilde. . . I know it was under false pretense. What was the purpose of such a spectacle?"

"They were directing you, it would seem. Frightening you back into your hole. . ."

"Borghild," Rathar whispered. "The bastard had me followed to Borghild."

"You see, yes yes, after I had reported seeing you in Lanthchilde, though it was at terrible risk following you to the castle, Merek's imposter followed you to Borghild with the intention to kill the Mistress Vivica. You see they are taking out your sources of protection one by one, or well, well, trying to."

"But to what end?" Rathar narrowed his eyes. "You certainly know a lot, magician."

"Once you choose sides, Rathar, you must put your skin in the game lest you lose it, you see. Now, now," he continued, "while you were most unfortunately *resting*, I contacted Mirabelle as she is, after all, under the assumption I've, well, chosen my side."

"And you told her what?" Rathar pressed, urgency in his voice.

"I made Mirabelle aware of Merek's death, *a truth*. I showed her your Stalker's banner and said that after the death of Vivica, you had killed Merek in despair and had found me in Adonica, and that I was treating your wounds. *A lie*. With the faux Merek dead, yes, yes, there is no one to confirm Gisela or Vivica are alive, she has only my word to go on." Wells sat back proudly and crossed his legs in front of the fire.

"You honestly think she fell for such a fool's trick?!" Rathar leapt up, and Wells feared he might come straight through the coals once more.

"You don't understand, Stalker," Wells put his hands up in defense, though in truth they'd be useless if it came down to it, "now she thinks that you're here idling your days in Adonica with the other Stalkers; your prophetess is, well well, quite dead, and that one of her biggest magical threats is neutralized. I simply knew you would never let me contact Mirabelle had I asked you. I thought you might not trust me."

Rathar inhaled sharply, and buried his face in his palms, calming himself forcefully. "I see what you did, Wells, I do, but from here on out, we need to approach things with a sense of collaboration. . . *without* rendering one another torpid or. . . any such thing." He closed his eyes tightly. "So, do you believe she was persuaded?"

"I believe so; but it will not be long before Gisela reaches Reliquary and the ruse is up. For now, Mirabelle believes me an accomplice to her malice. Let us hope she leaves us well enough alone through my crystal."

"She thinks Vivica is dead, but Viv. . . she's moving about the Provinces freely and *very much alive*." He glared at Wells for a moment, regretting having ended up in this convoluted nonsense. "Wait!" This time Rathar did come straight through the coals, stomping the flames near out with his boots. "You have a crystal ball? Wells, I need to see that!" Rathar grasped the shining sphere hungrily out of Wells's outstretched hands and focused very carefully as he looked deep into the swirling centre. He practically shouted the mustering incantation and focused his mind on Vivica, hoping dearly she was near enough her own crystals to know he was trying to contact her.

"Rath, where are you? This is no common Diviner's ball you're reaching me from. Have you met Luanda?"

"What? Luanda? No. Vivica, listen, don't be upset, but we couldn't haunt Adonica any longer. Gisela went ahead."

"Rathar! You needed a magician! I sent one, but I told you to wait and be patient." Vivica was vexed and that was the politest way to put it.

"I found a magician, Viv, we figured it all out. Not just why Gisela shifted, but how, and how she could do it again; I felt she was safe to go on. That, and we found her. . . well, call it a bodyguard. Myself and the magician have headed west to help with the aspirmeyg issue; I assume you've heard by now."

"Yes, I've heard. It's quite the talk now, when one isn't wrapped up in Consortium business. This is an earful you have given me, Rath. I have sent my own magician, a *trusted* one."

"I don't tend to trust any of the bastards of the Consortium, Vivica, and I can't sit around in Adonica, I'm roaming. Listen to me; you need to lie low, as low as possible, preferably six feet under." He scoffed at the absurdity of his request.

"What are you talking about?"

"I'm not sure how to put this judiciously, Viv, but you're supposed to be dead right now. You need to get to Borghild and seek the safety of its secret; I killed the only outsider to ever find it, so you needn't worry." Rathar was speaking frantically.

"Rathar. My darling, I need you to speak calmly and relate to me what has happened." Vivica's words were like a spell, in fact they probably were. Rathar inhaled deeply and told her all that Wells had made known to him.

Vivica stood still and cold as stone. She nodded gravely after considering Rathar's words. "I will seek Borghild, and I will not be found, but dear, I will have to emerge and make a move soon enough. I don't know what is happening in the Provinces these days exactly, but I do know that it will take all of us to make it right."

"I'll check on you, Viv. It'll be alright." Rathar was firm.

"Oh my darling, if I could but kiss your head and tell you the same. But look at you, a strong and capable man now who no longer needs the vows of the Mistress of Borghild," she sighed slightly, "please Rathar, wait for my confidante, Luanda, I plead with you. At least send her back safely."

"Where are you, Viv?"

"Never mind me, wait for Luanda and then make your way back to Borghild. We will decide what to do there." The crystal suddenly went dark, and Rathar furrowed his brow.

"You have no intention of doing either of those things, Rathar? No, no, I don't suppose you do."

Rathar handed the ball back to Wells. "We must be very careful with that, Wells. It's our lifeline."

"Yes, yes, and very well our doom."

Chapter

14

VIVICA ARRIVED AT THE TOWER of Gundrada under the dim starlight, and approached the tall, splintered wooden doors in the cover of near darkness. She was appropriately clad in a shadowy, brocade cloak with black fur that lined the sleeves and hood. One never had to sacrifice style for practicality she always said, and her figure was expertly hidden under the sable folds of fabric and fur.

"Master Orien isn't in," a royal guard dressed head to toe in plated armour and carrying a fearsome looking cleaver announced.

"Take ya round back though, help ya out of those furs. Let's see what pretty face is hidin' under that hood, eh?" the other guard chortled.

"I said, Master Orien isn't in. We guard these doors, and we ain't movin'." The first guard impressed, knocking the other guard in the helmet. "Not even for no *beautiful* woman." He smirked.

"Oh." Vivica's dark lips twisted into a devilish smile. "I wasn't asking gentlemen." She opened her hand to reveal in her palm a small handful of smooth obsidian stones, and with a short incantation her palm sparked wildly though it did not burn, and the treasures began to smoke tremendously. She puffed her cheeks and blew the smoke into the faces of the two guards who began to choke and spit before falling into a limp heap of bodies and armour on the ground. "Don't worry, dears, you won't remember a thing." Vivica muttered another spell under her breath and threw open the doors in a rush of cold wind. The tower was void of its resident; she knew this. Orien was to be in Reliquary making arrangements for his arrival. In this sleepy town, he need only lock his doors to keep unwanted visitors away. Never would he have expected the intrusion of another magician, especially not after having demonstrated his authority at the summit of the northwestern magicians, indeed to all of the Consortium. They trusted each other too much; she scoffed and whipped her arms from beneath her cloak whispering an incantation to wipe away all trace of her presence behind her, including the intoxicating smell of evergreen. Vivica climbed the spiral stair and brazenly let herself into Orien's chamber, scattered with stacks of books and littered everywhere with papers and half packed poplar trunks. Though Orien wouldn't have expected any sort of common thief, he certainly wasn't stupid; anything of import or undisclosed information would be hidden. It would take great potential to perform that kind of finding magic, to break those types of protective hexes. The greatest potential in the room was herself; she would have to use that to her advantage. It wasn't a type of magic that was admired or revered, in fact, it was considered very grave to use blood magic when still in good standing with the Consortium, but Vivica could do the math, and there was no other powerful potential to draw on that could break Orien's spells, could reveal his secrets. She reached into the folds of her cloak and pulled out a small dagger with a red stone laid into the hilt and made a deep cut in the palm of her hand which she used to smear a fret onto the floor, a symbol that would be a conduit for her spell. All she required now was the potential for the magic to feed on. She pulled up the hem of her dress and tucked it into her belt and stood in the center of the fret, making two deep cuts in the sides of her thighs letting the blood run freely down her legs and onto the floor. It pooled at her feet, and she grew dizzy, head dancing, and the lines of the room growing soft as if she were dreaming. "I'll find your secrets, you bastard." She groaned and the fret began to glow as she staggered to her knees. "Nearly there." The blood was warm and sticky in her boots; she could feel it squelching between her toes. *It's too much. I'm losing too much*, she thought. Suddenly she heard a voice, Orien's voice. It filled the room with mutterings, questions, concerns. "That's it! He's hidden his very thoughts with protective spells. Very clever, old magician. But I've discovered them." Vivica crumpled to the floor atop the fret and closed her eyes both trying to focus and because she was finding it difficult to keep them open. She listened to his secrets, and her lips twisted into a smile, a forbidden victory.

15

GISELA GRIMACED IN HER SLEEP and curled up tightly on her cot on the floor as Tycen adjusted the wrappings gently on her arm. It had been a rather gruesome affair resetting the bone back in place, and the sedative of lemon balm and lavender, though a crude supplement by Tycen's own admission, had made her drowsy. "Don't get me wrong, I'm happy to be rid of that tavern; a corse always stifles the energy, but I have to say, is this the best we could do?" Tycen looked around the Temple but only briefly as he noticed the hard stare of a Stalker on his back.

"Listen, Ranger," Quilla leaned into Tycen's ear and whispered, "nobody is gonna find us in here after killing that fat bastard, and we're even lucky that Arlen guy even let us in, thank God Sela's bone was sticking out like that, totally gross though, but the man has a soft spot for her, so this is as good as it gets." Tycen put his hands up in mock defense. "But listen, thanks. . . for everything. This is pretty bad, her being broken to shit like this; I kind of can't tell you why, but how long do you think she will take to heal up?"

"It's actually quite remarkable. . . the bone was healing as I was setting it. . . some sort of magic maybe?"

"Rathar!" Quilla practically jumped off her cot with joy.

"Who?"

"I'd have to kill ya." She winked.

"So, what's this proposition you have, Quilla?" Tycen leaned back against the wall resting his hands behind his head, glancing down every now and then at Gisela's arm rising and falling on her chest with her breath.

"What kind of life are you living right now, Ranger? Huh? Pretty boring I'd wager."

"Hah!" Tycen couldn't help himself. "Well, I can say that with all this aspirmeyg business taking place, my travels aren't as far and wide as they once were. Not only have they ravaged the Adonican Valley, but they sequestered my home on the Scaenus Plains as well. What do you want to wager we'll see them as far north as the Woods of Nurillia next."

"Well, I'd like to offer you some use, but first I've got to know, young man, whose side are you on?"

"Side?"

"You know. Everyone's got one."

"I suppose. . . I'm on my own side. That's the ranger way. You look out for yourself and those you owe."

"Well, you are in my debt."

"I'm *what*!?" Tycen chuckled.

"Earlier at the apothecary, I let you live. So, you're on my side because you owe me."

"I seem to recall me letting you live and fixing up your friend here."

"Alright so we owe each other which still puts us on the same side." Quilla shrugged.

"You haven't answered my question. What's the proposition?"

"I'm responsible for getting this lady here to Reliquary unscathed."

"You're doing well." Tycen smirked, and Quilla glared at him.

"She has a bit of a. . . well, a condition that I think could benefit from the hands of an herb man. Not to mention you're clearly useful with a weapon. What do you say to that?"

"How do you know you can trust me?"

"You haven't killed me. In my line of work, most people I can't trust try to kill me as a general rule."

Tycen smiled and made an apologetic gesture. "I'm sorry, Quilla, but I'll have to decline. I have my own business to see to. In fact, once your friend here wakes from her sleep, and I can examine her injuries, I should be on my way. But as a favour, I'll do you something customary of my people." Quilla's eyes grew big in anticipation. "Your horse out there, his leg looks a little tight; there is a way to massage it that will make him swifter to ride. I'll do that for you before I take my leave."

"You don't mean that grumpy no-named beast out there? I don't think he'd take too kindly to a rubdown from a stranger."

"I have a way with horses."

"Wait. . ." Quilla jumped up and covered her mouth to muffle her scream as not to wake Gisela. "You're not really. . . it isn't true. . . you're not. . . a Hisanrial!"

"In the flesh." Tycen grinned, stood up, and dusted his trousers with his calloused hands.

"Show me how you rub a horse!" Quilla eagerly followed him out of the Temple.

'The magicians are dividing up the Provinces; they haven't done that in a century at least; but they say this time Orien means to rehabilitate the Great City since Bernion always had his head in the sand. Starting with running the Hisanrial off the plains; you know what that means, that drossy lot will be filling our towns with their horse stink,' a man with a flattened cap moaned, passing the two and their horses outside the Temple.

Suddenly Tycen's friendly disposition turned sour and he spat angrily on the ground.

"Ch'aat," he hissed.

"What's that mean?"

"It's slander in horseman's speech. Those no-good magicians are dividing up the Provinces and driving us out of our homes. That's really why I'm here, Quilla. Some of us are trying to get a few supplies for our people, some of whom are dying, forced off our land. They're pushing us closer and closer to aspirmeyg territory, taking our native lands, and for what? So the Consortium can be richer than ever?" He spat again.

"Well, well, well." Quilla crossed her arms and grinned wide. "I'm feeling a little more generous with information mister ranger, and I have a feeling you're going to like what I have to say. You know who's the real *ch'aat*? Orien, formerly of Gundrada, presently of Reliquary, and he's gonna be a roast pig on a spit when we're done with him."

"You're going after the magicians that did this?" Tycen's eyes lit up.

"Spoken like a true hit man." Quilla giggled and began to recount her entanglement with Gisela and Rathar from the beginning, speaking in hushed tones.

"You're a noble woman, Quilla of many blades. I *will* join you. I owe it to my family before our way of life is erased."

"Yes!" Quilla punched the air, spooking Lief though he was easily soothed by a single, mysterious word from Tycen. "I assume you come with your own horse. Is it true you can stand on your hands while bareback at a canter? Is it true that—"

Tycen shook his head and walked into the temple to check on Gisela.

By morning Gisela's arm had healed with nothing left but a superficial mark and some lingering pains.

"You heal like a Stalker." Tycen grinned. Gisela's eyes grew wide, but Quilla laughed reassuringly.

"Sela, this is Tycen, he's a Hisanrial, that's truly amazing but beside the point; he'll be joining us on our travels, and he knows, well, he knows everything."

"Everything?"

"Everything I do."

"Oh, Quill. . ." Gisela stood up quickly with what could only be described as panic on her face.

"We can trust him."

"You can trust me." Tycen gently stepped forward and reached for Gisela's arm. "I did tend to you after all." Gisela blushed and extended her arm.

"It smarts a bit, but I think. . . well," she said after some consideration, "I think Rathar's power allows me to heal like he can."

"I'd say so." Tycen rubbed a strong, root smelling salve on Gisela's arm. "This should ease the remaining ache." Then he picked up his pack and shouldered it. "Reliquary won't be there forever, girls. Not if Orien is in charge. We'd best be on our legs."

"I like him." Quilla shrugged and picked up her belongings.

"I suppose I've always known the Hisanrial to be friendly before. . ."

"That's the spirit! And anyway, we need an herb man to help you shift, so get friendly, yourself." Quilla clapped her on the back and the three headed out of the temple. Gisela blessed Arlen, and Quilla for good measure and good fun, and the trio mounted their horses and headed north. "Hey, why didn't you get a blessing, Tycen? You know that Gisela represents God, don't you?"

"The Hisanrial," Tycen smiled politely, "believe in their own gods."

"But you've shared your table with the Hisanrial, Sela, at the Abbey, you said so!"

"Just because one is different to us, does not mean we cannot share our table." Gisela nodded seriously.

"Except Orien and his lackeys; they want us dead. We aren't sharing dog scraps with them!" Quilla laughed.

"I've even shared my table with those who have wanted me dead," Gisela mused.

"What happened?" Quilla turned around in the saddle.

"I. . . he died." Gisela sounded sad remembering Merek's dead weight in her lap.

"Well then that has been Orien's mistake, hasn't it?" Tycen chimed in, but his face was hard. They rode on in silence for a while, pensive. The cool morning turned into afternoon and the sun was bright and the sky clear above them; it made for a beautiful ride. Gisela admired the flora along the road and the way it was bathed in the light of the day, each tendril and riffle glowing under the beaming warmth. Tycen wanted to stop eventually, pointing out that he had spotted some plants growing that would make some helpful potions to aid the process Stalkers called shifting that wracked Gisela's more fragile body. He went to work picking and plucking while Gisela and Quilla soaked in the sunlight, patting the horses and running their fingers through their manes. Gisela let her gaze fall on Tycen, tenderly brushing soil from roots and petals and her mind was brought sweetly to Rathar, the way he used to amble through the woods and point out to her plants and their many properties. She remembered how he would crush the leaf of something and put it under her tongue, telling her all the while of its benefits, and she would squirm at the bitter taste. Gisela imagined for a moment that Tycen's bistered hands were Rathar's alabastrine ones, and she watched them untroubled until suddenly she went very still as if listening; she could feel something deep inside of her, a sense of sorts, telling her something was near. It wasn't her Vestal's gifts, it was something different, something so innate she was engulfed in it.

"Someone approaches."

"What do you mean?" Tycen stood, fistfuls of grasses in his hands. "This path is a ranger's secret, it's not likely we'd find anyone out here. . . "

"No, I think it's an aspirmeyg; I think I can sense it, actually feel its presence."

"Why couldn't you do that before?" Quilla punched her shoulder.

"Maybe I just didn't have the focus, but there's definitely one here, yes," she inhaled deeply through her nose, "I can smell it." A jolt of excitement rang though her voice.

"Can we avoid it?" Tycen shoved the verdure into bags quickly and rejoined the trio. Gisela paused for a moment. What would Rathar want her to do? Go the other way as quickly as possible, surely. The aspirmeyg was out in the wild, causing no real damage. . . yet. Perhaps it was best to go as far around as they could.

"We go around." Gisela nodded.

"We kick it's arse!" Quilla shouted, and the two looked at her as if she'd gone mad. "Listen, we're on the edge of Hisanrial territory. Territory that those bastard magicians are squashing every day and bringing closer to these aspirmeygs. Who is to say if we don't take care of this one it doesn't take care of somebody else tomorrow, Sela?" Gisela was troubled, and Tycen was silent for a moment.

"You're not supposed to hunt." He sighed, torn between his people and his charge.

"I would say these are extenuating circumstances." Gisela smiled and mounted Lief. "This way." Her confidence inspired her companions, and they followed swiftly through the forest, all but forgetting the loveliness of the day. As Gisela followed her senses and grew closer to the aspirmeyg, she allowed herself to shift; though it was not apparent under her billowing, wheaten robes, the contusion-like marks began to cover her body like a plague and slowly hindering her normal vision were thick, corded tendrils of tissue leaving only her superior Stalker's sense of smell behind. Suddenly, she halted the riding party shortly before a clearing of trees and pointed to a hulking creature curled in on itself surrounded by cloud-like stones in the middle. "A Boreas," she whispered. "It seems dormant. I can sneak up on it." Gisela slowly slid the bronze blade from her side and silently dismounted, signaling for Tycen and Quilla to remain where they were. Her heightened senses led her onward into the clearing, and she got daringly close, drawing the blade above her head to slice down across the dormant Boreas's back, but as she got close, she noticed something she hadn't before, her Stalker's senses made way for her Vestal's gifts and she saw, as if by her mind's eye, or perhaps more accurately her heart's, a black ether foaming in the belly of the beast, black magic. This Boreas wasn't dormant, it was enchanted; it was learning magic, but it was still vulnerable. Gisela slashed in her confusion again and again, across the back of the beast, and when it fell backwards into the soft grass, she slashed across its mangey belly spilling purple blood onto the forest floor. Gisela fell to her knees and pressed her thumbs to her eyes eagerly. For a moment she wanted to shift back; she wanted to forget what she had witnessed, forget the responsibility of it all, she wanted to stand in the sun again and relieve the burdens that now rested on her shoulders, but as the pains of shifting began to wrack her body, her fantasies left her mind and she called out for Quilla and Tycen.

"Shit, Sela. . . you kind of. . . massacred this thing." Quilla tiptoed around the pooling threads of blood and cut up, wisping Boreas parts that laid in a heap in the clearing while Tycen prepared a remedy for Gisela.

"Listen," she winced and tried to stand up.

"Easy, here take this." Tycen handed Gisela an expertly crafted pain draught and Gisela downed it in one swig.

"I saw something terrible, something incriminating, but to whom I can't say for certain. We have to talk to Rathar and Wells."

"Well, we can't just call them up with a crystal ball now, can we? Anyway, what is it?" Tycen steadied Gisela's delicate frame with his sturdy one.

"Black magic. That aspirmeyg wasn't dormant at all, it was under a spell, black magic."

"Black magic is outlawed by the Consortium. It has been for ages," Tycen challenged.

"It *was* enchanted. My Vestal's gifts, they see these things."

"Boy, you have a real confidence in justice and order, don't you?" Quilla rolled her eyes. "Anyway, who would enchant a killer to kill. . .?" She looked annoyed

"Except to kill specifically," Tycen added.

"To. . . to raise an army." A shiver went down Gisela's spine. "Maybe that's why aspirmeygs are amassing in the west. . . Orien's *magic* to contain them was magic to control them all along. The division in the Consortium trying *new magic*. . . it's black magic under wraps, and they're collecting an army of aspirmeygs to. . . Oh, God." Gisela wavered and fell hard to the ground, tears stinging in her eyes.

"Sela! What is it?!" Quilla knelt beside her, wiping the tear from her cheek with a calloused hand.

"The clearest, open path to Reliquary is from the west. Orien's not going to take over Reliquary like some Lord. . . he's going to. . . he's going to destroy it! He said to Rathar and me before, how he hated hope; how he desired to crush it." Tell me, she sobbed, "What's the brightest symbol of hope in all the Provinces but Reliquary and the Vestals it contains!? It stands between him and power." She buried her head in her hands. "They're just Vestals! They're defenseless against so many aspirmeygs, especially ones enchanted with *black magic*!"

"What do they possibly think they're going to do with the Stalkers?" Tycen scoffed.

"I don't know how, but I think they mean to overwhelm them." Gisela's eyes grew big. She feared for Rathar suddenly, alone fighting untold numbers of enchanted aspirmeygs every day. How she wished that she could see him, touch his face, hear his voice, truly know that he was okay. This was the first time in her travels that she felt that she truly missed him. Perhaps this was the first time she had time to miss him.

16

"HAVE YOU NOTICED THESE NUMBERS?" Rathar squinted over a little ledger by firelight. "I certainly try not to go, go through your things, Stalker." Wells smiled and Rathar glared hard at him for a moment, still tender from the previous altercation of being drugged and ransacked.

"In the last two months, I've killed one hundred and forty-four aspirmeygs, Wells."

"Yes, yes, it's a miracle you're still in one piece."

"Hardly. That's not the point. It's always between the hours of midmorning to sundown, they're always travelling west, and it's a variety of types. Never in my career have I ever seen all types of aspirmeygs in this area, on a schedule, travelling in a notable direction. It's like they're, well this sounds. . ."

"Enchanted," they both said together after a long pause.

"Lend your ear, the last time I worked with an aspirmeyg 'on a schedule' was with Orien. Fishy. And he had been trying to enchant the thing or something similar. I'm saying. . . what if he found a way? What if these aspirmeygs are. . . what if we're dealing with magic?" Rathar kicked his heels into the sward. "I should have dealt with that bastard then and there," he growled. "Choked the life out of him and took an extra piece of silver for the road."

"Don't fool yourself, Rathar. Orien let you walk free that day. In any case, we'd be wise to contact Vivica, yes yes, I'd say she'd better know about this right away, Rathar." Wells peered over his large spectacles into his bag and pulled out a crystal ball gleaming in the firelight. He handed it to Rathar, and it was cold and heavy in his hands which were tired from swinging his ponderous blade day after day. He held the crystal ball firmly in one hand and placed the other on top, reciting the incantation he'd memorized since boyhood, and focused all his thoughts on Vivica and Borghild until the swirling image of the Mistress of the Keep became clear in the glass. Her lips were pursed, and she looked less than happy to see him.

"Vivica, listen we have news." Rathar stifled a chuckle. "Do you sit in front of those damned crystals all day? I was sure we'd have no luck in reaching you."

"You should be here in Borghild. As I told you to be two months ago. We were to make plans, and I dared not contact you in case someone had come into possession of your crystal ball; I'm supposed to be *dead, remember?*"

"Vivica, I couldn't just leave the Valley. I've killed a hundred and a half aspirmeygs, and I've gathered intelligence."

"Let a mother scold every once in a while," she snapped. "You very well could have told me."

"I'm sorry Viv, but listen, these aspirmeygs, of all varieties, they're not typical. They're on a schedule, travelling in a fixed direction." Rathar felt something pop in his lumbar. "Right bastards to kill. Wells and I think they're enchanted somehow. It's just not right."

"You're right, I'm afraid. And I think the denouement is in the split of the Consortium. While I was in Gundrada poking around, I discovered convictions personal to Orien, spells and experiments. No doubt he was coming back for them with the rest of his effects, but he's been practicing black magic, more than just a dalliance. I suspect such applications and fancies have gained followers in the Consortium; I suspect that's what caused the split, and I deeply suspect there is something foul afoot, especially if they're enchanting aspirmeygs." Vivica sighed deeply.

"I feel powerless, Viv, waiting on Gisela. I've sent her to her death, almost certainly, and I've no way to help. If I could figure out where the aspirmeygs are travelling—"

"That's far too dangerous, darling; you'd be greatly outnumbered in such a situation."

"If I may be so bold, yes, yes, perhaps it's time for that family reunion," Wells stammered. "Pardon the interruption, my Lady," bowing gracefully to the crystal. Rathar and Vivica paused for a moment in thought.

"Not bad, Wells, not bad at all. I'd be outnumbered, sure, but if I could round up a group of Stalkers to follow the aspirmeygs, we could see where they're going."

"Rath, just remember, if they're enchanted with black magic; they're dangerous." Vivica looked stern.

"One hundred and forty-four. Remember *that*." He scoffed and bade farewell to Vivica, tucking the diaphanous ball back into the woolen sack.

"Rathar of Borghild," came a shrill voice from the dark behind them. Rathar and Wells jumped up into the dark, tripping over the hot coals in alarm.

"Who's there?" Rathar growled and quickly but clumsily drew his blade from the grass near his feet. He wasn't usually caught so off guard, but his conversation with Vivica had left him enraptured in his thoughts. Slowly from the darkness around them emerged a small figure, hooded and cloaked in black wool; she was covered head to toe with nothing to distinguish herself but a large emerald ring on her hand until she pulled back her hood to reveal cropped blonde hair framing the most delicate features. She smiled and held out her dainty hand in greeting.

"I apologise for appearing in the dead of night, Rathar, but you see I must avoid detection, if I can."

"Luanda, is that you?" Rathar said in utter surprise.

"I've been looking for you." Luanda smiled in a sweet and genuine way; it almost put Rathar at ease, a magician's trick surely. "Though I was told you would be in Adonica. When I couldn't find a trace of you there, I was most certain you'd be here with your brothers in the Valley. I come with instruction from Vivica whom you have made deceased, unfortunately." She bit her lip in a childish way. "Or else she would have run the errand herself."

"I don't make a habit of taking magicians as guests." Rathar eyed Luanda suspiciously.

"Come Rathar, I've known you since you were a boy."

"You must understand my position, Luanda. Magic hasn't been friendly to me these days," Rathar rasped.

"I was also told you were in need of a magician. It seems however that Gisela is not present as she was meant to be." Luanda scanned the campsite to confirm. "You're tensed up as stone. I'm not going to cast a spell on you, turn you into some sort of animal." She smiled pleasantly. "I've come a long way for this errand, Rathar; I've risked very much to make myself known to you."

"We have a magician. Wells here is our magician. He's done his duty, and we don't require a witch."

"Now, now, Rathar, there is no need to be disparaging." Wells stood and placed a hand on Luanda's shoulder. Rathar pursed his lips.

"I'm sorry. Sit. Stay," he grumbled reluctantly. "If you were sent by Vivica then you are a. . . a friend."

"I'm afraid I have other places to be, little Stalker, if I may still call you that." Luanda winked. "But I suppose I can stay for a short reprise." Luanda sat next to Rathar and leaned forward breathing onto the fire with a gentle puff; suddenly it roared and crackled anew, and she sat back comfortably. "I was afraid I wouldn't recognise you, but that fiery hair, well, I couldn't miss it, could I? And now you're all grown-up with whiskers to match." Luanda smiled.

"I suppose it has been a great length since we've seen each other, Luanda. I apologise for my mistrust."

"Vivica always instructed you to be chary. She imparted many wisdoms to you, Rathar. Do not forget them in your present situation."

"I wasn't prepared for anything such as this. I was prepared for a simple life of putting beasts to the sword. I wasn't meant to lose anyone," Rathar mumbled.

"Do you remember when you took your oath? I was there that day. It was in late spring. The irises were in bloom, and they swayed in the breeze."

"The irises in the garden used to give me a rash. I always found them ugly after that."

"You are like vinegar in sweet wine; do you know that?" Luanda laughed. "Anyway, it's not about the irises. It's about the oath itself. Do you remember what Vivica told you, after you'd pledged yourself to the protection of the Provinces?"

"Like it was yesterday, only it was years and years ago, now. She said 'onward to better men, and do not count the cost.'"

"You would be wise to remember those words now, little Stalker. This trial may yet be for the good of the Provinces; you know not when a prophecy is involved. If it involves those you care for, then it most certainly makes you a better man, and you need not count the cost because you have never been in that business." Luanda touched Rathar's hand. Rathar pursed his lips. The magician was right. "Now, if my services are not needed, I must leave you before I compromise the situation. Farewell." Luanda concealed herself with her cloak once more and slipped back into the darkness.

"Vivica takes great risk sending errand girls, and who knows what she overheard," Rathar grumbled. "She didn't seem to know you, Wells; are you not acquainted?" he asked.

"No no, I'm afraid not, but if Vivica sent her, we can surely trust that she doesn't keep sour company."

"For now, we trust the Luanda of my youth," Rathar sighed. "Wells, we'd better get some sleep. Tomorrow we're due for a little family reunion." Wells gulped hard. He knew the notorious repute Stalker's had; he'd been thoroughly spoiled to travel in the company of Rathar and Gisela.

"Yes, yes," Wells said and felt his stomach turn a bit queasy, "I'm sure I'll sleep a spell."

The next morning finally brought leave of the weathered campsites Wells and Rathar had called home for nearly two months; they packed up their things and headed further westerly in an effort to pluck up as many Stalkers as they could, scattered across the Adonican Valley. They'd all lived very much the same for the past few months, making camp in the Valley and intercepting aspirmeygs as they headed across the grassy basin during the light hours of the day. Rathar had even bumped into a few Stalkers on the hunt, exchanging nothing more than a, "Isn't this bullshit?" and a couple of meager supplies, but at least he knew they were out there to find and relatively close together. A Stalker wasn't something he could use his senses to track, the bastards never smelled like fear; they feared almost nothing in this life, but a semipermanent campsite and a man that hadn't bathed in an eternity? That had to be easy enough.

"We'll keep to the main road for now. I know Arkyn's camp is somewhere off this road, he told me about it when I bought a few tinctures off him last month."

"I say, Rathar, what, what is that up there?" Wells swung his arm up over his eyes to block out the morning sun and nearly lost his balance, his apothecary pack was so laden with the treasures of two months' work. "Is it dangerous?" Far ahead at a knotted old pine was a slumped black heap. "Well I say, surely you, you, can see!" Rathar glanced up and immediately his voice was stuck in his throat.

"They knew we'd come this way." Rathar choked out in a low voice. What he saw was a gruesome display. A woman lay in a pile of her own viscous entrails, the dirt of the path was still warm and sticky with her blood, and her head was missing. Leaving a swarm of black flies at the stump of her neck and belly.

"Who is this woman?!" Wells pinched his nose at the smell and swatted at the flies. Rathar gently moved the woman's hand away from her crumpled body with his boot to reveal a familiar, gargantuan emerald ring.

"Luanda. She was being followed. They knew we'd come this way, and they made a sign of her, a warning." Wells blanched at the thought. "Headless and gutted," Rathar scoffed. "Someone thought they were being funny. A Stalker's bread and butter." Wells had begun to sweat profusely. "Mirabelle knows you're with me, and she feels she has some semblance of control over that, but when she caught wind of Luanda sneaking around, she must have had someone follow her. Sure enough, as soon as she discovered that Luanda intended to assist us, she wanted to send us a message: the Consortium isn't safe. The question is, did they get any information out of her before they killed her?"

"Rathar, we'd better get out of sight." Wells shivered.

Rathar nodded gravely, and for a moment he thought he might pray for the dead magician, but it was a passing fancy, and the words never came to him, so he shouldered his bag and they continued on the path with the intention of using more caution than before, though he couldn't help but to let his mind wander to Gisela. Sometimes he wondered if she was even alive, but he scolded himself for thoughts like that. She had to be, surely if he could share something so close with her as his powers, he would *know* if she were gone; he could feel and sense so many things, surely he would feel and sense something so grave so. . . heartbreaking. Caution. The way her golden curls framed her face when she smiled. Vigilance. The way her chest rose and fell as she slept and dreamed; he always wondered what she dreamed about, but he never asked. Soon, it was like he was in a dream himself, remembering simpler times, looking forward to reuniting, not caring where his feet took him.

"Who goes?" came a gruff voice from a clump of leafy aspens. Suddenly, Rathar snapped out of his lovely dream and cursed himself for his lack of vigilance.

"Arkyn, it's Rathar." Rathar retrieved from his pack the crimson banner ornamented with the golden scorpion's tail and held it out in front of him. "The herbalist is my companion." Arkyn said nothing but nodded his head and led them into the thicket. To Rathar's surprise, it was not the camp of a single Stalker, but there were five others with Vestals to match sitting around a campfire ring tending to various injuries, eating, and grunting in a way that clearly intimidated Wells. "I don't understand. We're not exactly. . . pack animals." Rathar furrowed his brow. One of the Stalkers looked up, and to Well's surprise, jumped up from where his Vestal had been wrapping a bandage on his leg.

He shouted enthusiastically, "Rathar you old rascal! It's been years! Where's that gorgeous thing of yours, you haven't gone and got her killed have ye?" He laughed from deep in his belly. "Tell me you bedded her before at *least*? I'm joking, I'm joking, those robes are shut tighter than a clamshell," he laughed again and elbowed Rathar hard in the ribs, very hard Wells thought. "Who's this wee man, and why is he sweating like that? Looks as slippery as a pig who knows it's about to be spitted!" he laughed thunderously.

"Dag." Rathar acknowledged the man without any expression. "Arkyn, what is everyone doing here? It certainly makes my job easier, but it's a recipe for disaster, if you ask me. How have you not. . . murdered each other?"

Arkyn clapped a tall girl in tawny Vestal's robes between the shoulder blades. "If it weren't for them, perhaps we might have. But we mostly keep to ourselves, gone all day killing those miserable devils, come back to sleep and eat. We're going through so many resources, it made sense to come together and pool them, for the time being. Damn it all, I don't think I can take much more to be honest, but the bastards keep coming. Surprised you made it this long on your own." One of the Stalkers scoffed in agreement, and another let slip a crude insult. "Have you come to join?"

"Not exactly. . . but I do need your help. Vivica needs us." At those words every Stalker stopped what he was doing and looked up at Rathar with full attention. They may have been rude, and sometimes savage men, but they had the utmost respect for the mistress of Borghild. Rathar began to relate all that he had noted about the idiosyncrasies of the aspirmeygs, and many of the Stalkers agreed that they, too, had noticed the odd behaviour, except for Dag who admitted he simply lived to "cut their damned throats and bleed 'em, and I don't care what time of day I be doin' it either."

"We can't just sit here on our arses as enchanted aspirmeygs amass in the west. We need to go look at where they're going, and I don't think it'd be wise to go alone. Vivica thinks we should all go together."

"Seven Stalkers. Better than one I'd say." Arkyn stroked his beard and looked down at his Vestal who nodded in agreement.

"Have you forgot the purity of our craft, boys? We're Stalkers. Life is plain as a beggar's frock for us. We kill aspirmeygs 'n take our pay from the Temple, and here in the Valley there are aspirmeygs to be killed. Do you know what kind of money the ledger-man will be handin' out to us in Adonica with work like this?" Dag threw his arms over his head in protest.

"The aspirmeygs are gathering rapidly, Dag. Soon there might not be an Adonica to dole out your silver," Rathar snapped.

"Oh, what? So you think war is comin' boy? With the aspirmeygs?" Dag laughed again from deep in his belly. "Listen to this, fellas! He don't need no Vestal. He thinks *for himself.*" Dag spat on Rathar's boots. "You know what they call this prick and his lassie in Reliquary? *The Chosen Pair.* Fodder." He wiped his nose on his sleeve and a few of the other Stalkers harrumphed. "What are you looking at, little man?" He glared at Wells, making himself look frighteningly large. Rathar put his bulking arm between Dag and Wells, and before he could retort, a very patient looking Vestal emerged from the crowd, still holding a bandage in her hand.

"Dag. Please. We don't have to go, but we shouldn't interfere. Especially in Vivica's affairs." Dag squinted his eyes and took a few staggering steps back from Wells.

"I say we go. It's what Vivica wants, and I'm damned tired of doing this day after day. Besides, we might get to the root of the problem." Arkyn motioned for the group to pack up. There were some grunts of affirmation and some low grumbles as Stalkers and Vestals convened to organize their scanty belongings.

"I won't do it." Dag argued. "It's a simple Stalker's life for me, thank you," he growled.

"Fine." Arkyn shrugged. "Rathar and his companion will take your horses." Dag's eyes narrowed but he dared not argue further with Arkyn, who clearly had established his dominance among the group.

•• ———— ••●•• ———— ••

Riding and camping in the company of his kin brought neither comfort nor nostalgia for Rathar, in fact, it was downright vexatious. The days were filled with growls, grunts, aggressive arguments, and physical altercations about whether to stay on the road, when to stop, and who should lead; the nights, of course, and much to the embarrassment of the present Vestals, though Rathar thought they had to be used to it by now, were filled with boisterous tales of bedding women. Wells was wholly out of his element though he was able to trade herbal expertise with a few out of the group that didn't look as though they wanted to tear apart his gaunt limbs and use them as toothpicks. After a few days of this, Rathar thought he might come unhinged, though all of the Stalkers started to become uneasy.

"Do you feel it?" Rathar trotted up to the front of the company where Arkyn looked deep in thought.

"Aspirmeygs, an abundance of them. We all sense it." Arkyn closed his eyes and inhaled deeply through his nose.

"Just over that ridge there. . . impossible. . . do you smell that? So many?"

"Only one way to find out." Arkyn motioned for the group to ride slowly to the ridge. They approached it by cover of a thicket of aspen trees which decorated the top of the ridge like an expensive jewel in a facet. When they peered out from their branchy shelter, the Stalkers were frozen in their saddles. Rathar let the breath escape his mouth in shock. Before them in a deep valley were hundreds of aspirmeygs of every variety arranged by type and lined up in battle formations.

"I think we found what we were looking for," Arkyn whispered gravely.

"It's a damned army." Rathar closed his eyes, but the sight was imprinted in his mind. "They're enchanted, after all, to form lines like soldiers."

"For what fuckin' purpose do you suppose?" another murmured from the back.

"There's one clear shot from here: Reliquary." Rathar felt his stomach drop as the realization of what he'd just said sank in. He turned around and saw the wide eyes of the Vestals behind him. Some began to well up with tears.

"Son of a bitch. We'd best get out of here," another Stalker urged.

"And go where?" said another. "Back to the Valley while they gather here to march on those poor lasses in the Great City?" The Stalkers were silent for a moment, taking in the consequence of the sight before them.

"We're going home. To Borghild. To prepare for war," Rathar rasped.

"There's only seven of us, you crazy bastard! We'll lose. You can bet your orange, hairy arse on that." One of the Stalker's grimaced.

"Arkyn, you know of more of us in the Adonican Valley?"

Arkyn nodded.

"Take two of the others and make haste from the Valley to Bero, there are sure to be more there. Find as many as you can and bring them back to the castle. We'll gather. We'll make a plan."

"Raud, Toril, you're swift riders. You're with me." Arkyn looked soberly at the Vestal riding beside him. "Sabrina. Don't fear for naught." He squeezed her shoulder reassuringly and the three riders and their accompanying Vestals hurried off back towards the Valley.

"As for the rest of you, we're headed north if you want a livelihood to come back to, and I won't hear shit about it," Rathar snapped and took the lead turning north toward Borghild, Gisela now the paramount consideration turning over and over in his mind.

Chapter

17

"THIS STRETCH OF ROAD IS familiar; I know by which way we come," Gisela mused as she dismounted Lief. "Good. You think long and hard on it, and I'm going to get some water from the stream. I'm parched." Quilla dismounted her own horse and grabbed the soft, leather canteen from her saddle horn.

"I'll come with you!" Tycen quickly hurried after, their laughter erupting into the trees, and Gisela could have sworn he'd blushed. Her heart sank as she spotted a sparse clump of winter heather growing near her feet, the beautiful purple plumes just enough to give it away. She breathed in the scent, now stronger and sweeter than ever before with her Stalker's senses, and she let it fill her up as if she had been empty and was now teeming and brimming with something familiar; it was something, or someone rather, she longed to grasp for and cling to, a sensation she let linger in her nostrils as long as possible, but the trance was soon broken by the sounds of emerging laughter through the trees once more.

"Sounds like you really gave him a run for his money! That reminds me of my first bounty." Quilla said proudly, "That's why the elves in Haleth call me 'the half-arrow demise'."

"You've done hits for the elves?"

"I'm one special lady." Quilla grinned a wide, toothy grin.

"You are that indeed." Tycen reached his hand to her face and softly brushed her hair behind her ear. He blushed like wine. Gisela cleared her throat, hiding her growing smile.

"Reliquary is days from here; we've lost some time *hunting* aspirmeygs." She swallowed hard on the word knowing what trouble she'd be in if Rathar ever found out. "But Tycen, you've been an invaluable help. The pain from shifting is so much more bearable with your remedies, and I'm going to need all of the energy I can get in Reliquary. . . it takes a lot to read a prophecy."

"What do you mean? You don't just pick it up. . . and. . . read it? Like a book or something?" Quilla queried.

"It's not quite that simple." Gisela shook her head, and her golden curls danced in the sunlight.

"I'm sure I could mix you up a supplement of sorts."

"None of that matters if we can't get in. We can't simply stroll through the ingress. Orien knows me. He's seen my face, heard my voice."

"He thinks you're dead," Quilla said.

"So, imagine if he sees me very much alive."

"That would present a problem, indeed. Where exactly are these prophecies kept?" Tycen had a glitter in his eye.

"At the Abbey, of course. There is a group of sacred Vestals who are borne with the task of both writing and keeping the prophecies. It is the only position a Vestal can inherit by birth."

"What if I could get in? The Hisanrial have been welcomed at the Abbey before in high regard. . . I could say I need to speak to the Abbess on urgent business and explain our predicament. She could give me the prophecy; I'd bring it back here, and you could read it with the help of my herbs."

"That's fantastic!" Quilla shouted, and Gisela threw a hand over Quilla's mouth.

"We are too near the enemy to be so careless, Quill." Quilla nodded apologetically. "Tycen, Orien is dangerous. He feigned weakness at my last encounter with him, but he has proven himself to be a powerful player. If something should happen to you. . ." Gisela leaned in close and whispered into Tycen's ear. His eyes widened and he took a few steps backwards bowing deeply to Gisela.

"Thank you for such a rare honour. I know you do not divulge such information unless the situation is most grave." Tycen reached into his bag and revealed a small copper pot that fit just in the palm of his hand, and he scraped out of the bottom a crimson paste smearing it across his cheeks and forehead in the traditional markings of the Hisanrial. "Look the part." He winked. "Wait for me here. I'll bring the prophecy back. I promise," he added, squeezing Quilla's hand as he mounted his horse and rode north.

•• ———— ••●•• ———— ••

Tycen had never been one of the Hisanrial to have the pleasure of seeing Reliquary before; it truly was the jewel of the Provinces, a place where the highest of scholarly pursuits met the roots of provincial religion. Reliquary was the fulcrum for Vestals and their creation; they were brought up and schooled at the grand Abbey there. A select few were matched with Stalkers for lives of adventure and peril. Some were prophecy keepers, an ancient and revered task. Others were in the occupations of academia or the clergy; whatever they did, Vestals were indispensable to the Provinces, and their city was as famous as they were. Reliquary had to be the most beautiful place he had ever seen, Tycen thought. The leviathan stone buildings almost blushed in the sunlight and had great archways with carved keystones the size of a man to match in the center of each. Schools maybe? Libraries? Everywhere he looked, underneath the flowering shade trees and strolling across the large lawns, were Vestals in wheaten robes, some carrying stacks of books, others holding hands and laughing. Peristyles and courtyards each encapsulating their own variety of orchard sprawled before various porticoes, entrances to buildings that enticed Tycen and piqued his interest, each one a mystery. He continued up the main gravel path until he reached a foreboding portcullis where two men who did not seem to belong were standing guard.

"What business do you have at the Abbey?" One demanded from under his shining helmet.

"Is the Abbess hiring out private security?" Tycen scoffed.

"Let me put it in a way you might understand horse-lover. The Hisanrial aren't welcome at the Abbey no more. Not since master Orien took over this Province," the other guard hissed. "He says no one in. And no one out." He added with a sinister grin.

"This is still my Abbey," came a booming voice from beyond the portcullis. "I will see my guests, unless you'd like it reported to Master Orien that you were sleeping on the job. . . again."

"No ma'am," chirred the first guard as he hoisted up the portcullis, slapping Tycen's horse on the rear and grinning so that a few of his rotten teeth showed.

"You must be the Mother Superior. . . erm. . . Abbess." Tycen dismounted and held out his hand, unsure if that was proper decorum for a Vestal.

"I was not expecting a messenger from the Hisanrial. To be quite frank, sir, I was not expecting anyone. We are not allowed many visitors anymore."

"Mother," Tycen lowered his voice as they entered the courtyard. For a moment he was distracted by its beauty. A mammoth stone fountain stood in the middle with clear water running down its sides. On the benches beside it sat a few younger Vestals; Tycen thought they still only must be children. They were exchanging fair flowers they had picked from the woods bordering the edge of the courtyard. Where old, moss-covered statues of nymphs had stood watch for eons. There were flower crows hanging from their stony fingers. *This is where Gisela must have played as a child.* He smiled. "We must speak somewhere private."

She nodded and led Tycen to her drawing room. It was quaint, he thought, in comparison to the grandeur of Reliquary, nothing more than a plain, wooden desk that sat in the middle of the room, unassuming to the background of peeling paint on the walls; clearly there were other tasks at the Abbey more important than inconsequential upkeep. Behind the desk was a creaking, old chair that threatened to fall apart as the Abbess sat in it a little too confidently, Tycen thought to himself. Peculiarly, though, there were no papers, scrolls, or records. The drawing room was all but bare.

"I see you snooping, oh master of horses." She smiled, and in the deep wrinkles on her cheeks Tycen saw what perhaps used to be dimples in her youth. He was abashed at his brazenness. "It's true I run a large establishment, a whole city. But what I need, *He* provides. All here. She pointed to her heart first and then to her head."

"You mean to say. . . if I may say, that is, great Mother, that all your records, everything is. . . *in your mind?*" Tycen felt his mouth drop open a little.

"By the power of God, every Abbess is allowed this rare gift." She smiled again. Tycen suddenly felt aware of the crimson paint on his face muddling with the blood rising to his cheeks, the ostentatious show of his own beliefs and gods, and for the first time in his life, he felt powerless. He wanted to test her, push her to her limits, but he remembered his mission and checked his pride.

"Mother, I'll be brief. Surely you know Rathar of Borghild and Gisela, one of your own."

"There are many who share the name Gisela here, but the one who travels with Rathar of Borghild, the Stalker. Yes. A rare pairing, indeed. Tell me, honourable Hisanrial," Tycen could tell she meant no flattery, "what business do you have with the chosen pair?"

"The. . . chosen pair?"

"Come, you must know that God is with them. Can you not tell that Rathar has no need of the Vestal's power? I imagine the prophecy waiting for them in the Ambry is something marked. I imagine, it will change the fate of these Provinces." Her voice turned downcast. "They need changing, horsemaster." Tycen made no mention of his unfamiliarity to Rathar lest it jeopardise his odds at getting the prophecy.

"Mother, I must tell you something." Tycen clenched his fists as he envisioned the untroubled girls by the fountain. "Orien is going to destroy Reliquary. War is coming." To his surprise she was not shocked, nor was she upset in any way. The old woman only smiled sadly at him.

"People see Vestals as indispensable to this world, noble horseman. But we are like everyone else at the end of all things, individual lives, no better than you, and with no higher purpose than any other being."

"But still worthy of life! This is genocide if he means to wipe you out!"

"And what can we do? Scholars, clergy, prophetesses. It's in your hands, Hisanrial." Mother stood from her chair and took Tycen's hands in her own wizened one ones, squeezing them tightly. It was something of a comfort as much as a call to action. "You are here for the prophecy. For Rathar's prophecy. I will give it to you. I ask you one thing in return, Hisanrial." She smiled and said simply, "Save us."

●● ———— ●●●●● ———— ●●

The Ambry was a beautiful room of stone and stained glass. Mother led Tycen in and showed him where young and old Vestals worked together; some were diligently writing as if in a trance, and some were placing and organizing beautiful amber bottles with scrolls concealed inside into stone cubbies along the walls so high and wide that a system of ladders had to be used to reach them.

"They're all unlabeled. How do you know what prophecy is for whom?" Tycen wondered aloud.

"Only the prophetesses can tell. In a way, that keeps the prophecies safe."

"In the case of Stalkers and Vestals. . . only the Vestal can read the prophecy. What for a common man? Who reads his prophecy? How does he know he's got one?"

"Only a Vestal you have a bond with can read your prophecy. Never fear, these bonds can be created through meditation and willing volunteers, but only once and with one single Vestal. It's like trapping a moth in your hands; you'd better make your wish before it flies away." Mother smiled and pointed to a small room to the side where a small altar was flanked with two kneeling cushions. "Most people never know they have prophecies their whole life long, and once the flame of their life is extinguished, so the prophetess extinguishes the prophecy, and it is often inconsequential." She shrugged. "It is the signs in life that signal one to the presence of a prophecy. You must be keen enough to seek it out, here in the humble Ambry of Reliquary." The Abbess nodded and motioned for one of the older Vestals to step away from her current task. She spoke with her in hushed tones, and the Vestal signaled compliance with a deep and respectful bow. The Vestal then walked over to the series of stone cubbies and began to scan with her eyes, quickly, flitting over the bottles with gentle fingers until she stopped on one as unassuming as the rest.

"Here it is." She bowed once more and presented the bottle to Tycen, lifting her sleeve to reveal the fullness of the golden glass. Tycen took it in a firm grip. It was quite possible that this was Reliquary's last lifeline now; it was obvious that Orien had never wanted Rathar to find it, and what was contained in this prophecy could be their last hope, could be the last hope for the Provinces, of his own people. His knuckles were white as he tucked the bottle into the leather bag at his side, concealing it under his Hisanrial's cloak.

"Go." Mother urged him from the Ambry. "You are not the only guest of honour here in the city today. Make no hesitations and you will not be stopped. Leave how you came in, noble horsemaster."

Tycen left the Ambry swiftly. He tried not to look conspicuous as he walked, quickly, through the raked gravel paths back toward his horse, dizzy with the sight of tawny robes hither and thither, trembling at the sound of innocent laughter and chatter. Soon it could be gone, blotted from the Provinces in one cruel massacre. *No*, he thought, *I don't know Rathar; I don't know what he's capable of, but it must be something great if this prophecy is so important. . . if they're the chosen pair. I must have hope.* Tycen tried to control his trembling, to direct his steps swiftly when he heard something behind that stopped him in an instant.

"Master Orien, the Abbess will see you shortly. This way." Tycen felt as though he would vomit and that a flame were ignited in his belly all at once, but he couldn't move. His feet were frozen in place. "Move, boy, you're in the way of the great magician. Are you deaf? Are you dumb?" The attendant kicked up gravel at Tycen.

"Stop. What is this Hisanrial doing here? I strictly permitted no guests in *my city*," Orien hissed. "Turn around, boy, we'll have a look at you." *Make no hesitations.* Tycen thought as he slowly turned around thinking of the amber bottle carefully tucked at his side, but when his eyes met the magician's, the fire in his belly coursed through every vein in his body like an inferno, and his hatred shone through his eyes as if he could cast spells of his own. Orien cackled wickedly. "Tell me boy, how many Hisanrial had to die before you came seeking charity from churchwomen?"

"You've pushed us to the edge of Scaenus," Tycen shouted. "My people are dying because you play with *maps and aspirmeygs!*" Concealed beneath his cloak, Tycen fingered the hilt of a dagger at his side.

"You've got an honourable tradition of fending for yourselves. Consider me an enabler." Tycen glanced around at the groups of Vestals who had gathered behind trees and stone porticoes looking on in apprehension. *Make no hesitations.*

"You murderous bastard!" He shouted and jutted forward, slicing at Orien with the dagger, but Orien stepped away, anticipating his recklessness. Tycen was enraged and careless with his movements. He leapt forward again stabbing this time toward Orien's chest, but Orien opened the palm of his hand and a forceful black ether knocked Tycen onto the ground; Orien clenched his fist, and Tycen was writhing in agony.

"Stop!" came a voice from the onlooking crowd. A Vestal who appeared to be the same age as Gisela with mousy, brown hair ran forward. "Stop! That's black magic! You're going to kill him!" She placed her hands on Tycen's thrashing body and began to recite prayers desperately, but they were to no avail. Orien released his fist, and Tycen's body relaxed for a moment, but just as the Vestal sighed in relief, he snapped his black, gloved fingers and the tanned, weathered skin of Tycen's throat began to bleed against her own pale hands. He choked and sputtered, gasping for air that would not come.

"Your God has no power here anymore." Orien motioned for his attendant to bring Tycen's horse to one of the Vestals, and he stepped carelessly over his dying body. "Send this beast back to the Hisanrial *without its rider*. A message to keep on my good side."

"I'm sorry," whispered the Vestal, as she applied pressure to Tycen's despondent wound. "I can't help you, I'm sorry." The other Vestals looked on in hopelessness. Courage would get them nowhere.

"Li. . . listen." Tycen expectorated bloody phlegm into the Vestal's hands and reached for the leather bag at his side, pushing it toward her. The Vestal pushed firmly on the wound and put her ear to Tycen's mouth. He sputtered his final words and went limp, no longer trying for breath or words. The Vestal gasped audibly and reached for the bag grasping it with sticky hands. She said one more prayer, kissing Tycen's forehead gently, a prayer of passing and then stood and seized the reins from the other Vestal nearby.

"Romilly, where are you going!?" the other Vestals called out. But Romilly secured the bag around her waist and climbed up onto Tycen's horse. With a shout she urged the horse onward at full canter and charged out of the city.

18

"**C**OME ON." GISELA GRINNED, "IT'S just us girls. Tell me, you're in love, aren't you?" Quilla poked the fire idly with a pine branch. "You do everything together!" Gisela smoothed out her robes matter-of-factly. "You collect water together, you gather firewood together, you hunt together, you. . ."

"Okay I get it!"

"And you're *always laughing!*"

"Hey! We aren't *always laughing.*" Quilla mocked Gisela's voice. "We talk. About things. Y'know. . . things I'm no good at, but he makes real easy." She chuckled and poked the fire again so that a plume of sparks rose into the darkness. "You know what, Sela? I've always felt like just *someone.* I'm just someone for hire y'know?

Don't get me wrong, someone with wicked skills, but I'm just *someone* who's bought out over and over again, for my skills." She sighed contentedly. "Tycen makes me feel like. . . *a woman*."

"Sounds like you've got yourself a puppy," Gisela giggled.

"Very funny!" Quilla grabbed her belly and laughed hard.

"I know how you mean. I don't even have skills." Gisela smiled weakly. "As far as Vestals go, I'm *useless*. Rathar doesn't need me to do my job. . . but he does *need me*, doesn't he? As a woman?" Gisela furrowed her brow as if she had thought about it that way for the very first time. "So." She leaned forward into the firelight and pinched her lips together. "Has he kissed you?"

"More like have *I* kissed *him*?! And aren't Vestals not supposed to talk about that kind of stuff anyway? Where do you get off?"

"I'm a Vestal in love, remember?" She winked.

"As if Rathar knows how to kiss a woman. I bet he couldn't kiss a frog with its big old lips," Quilla said flatly, and they both burst into joyous laughter. "Tell me, Sela, how did you and Rathar come to be anyway? How do Stalkers and Vestals get paired off in the first place? Draw straws?"

Gisela smiled softly. "There are a fair few of us always trained in time with the Stalkers at Borghild. As they are raised up from boys to defend the Provinces, we are raised up from girls for the same purpose; that's why we are roughly the same age. And then, when the time is right, the dear Abbess prays very much before she dispatches us with our new. . . family."

"But she doesn't even know the Stalkers! How can she make the best choice? Though I guess they're all the same, really, aren't they?"

"Are they, Quilla, all the same? I would say Mother's prayers put me right where I belong, wouldn't you?" Quilla's mouth widened a little in wonder. She intended to say more but was interrupted by the ripping and cracking of branches in the distance.

"That sounds like a horse!" Gisela jumped up.

"With an iron up the arse, I'd say!" Quilla clapped her hands together. Gisela raised a brow. "Quickly. . . It's coming quickly," Quilla clarified.

"Gisela!" shouted a voice from the forest. "Gisela is that you?!" Both the girls' eyes grew wide, and they grabbed their weapons in haste. "Gisela!" Suddenly a horse and rider tore through the foliage revealing what to Gisela was a familiar face.

"Romilly!" she nearly screamed.

"Oh, Gisela! I've been looking for you for days!" Romilly jumped off of the horse and embraced Gisela tightly.

"Romilly, eat and drink! God, you're not accustomed to the wilderness, you're a scholar! What an errand must have brought you out here!" Gisela took Romilly by the hand and led her to the warmth of the fire where she handed her a flask of water and some food. "I'm sorry. . . I know it's meat, but it's all we have." Romilly didn't seem to mind. She devoured it with a ravenous hunger. "You poor thing, you must be near death out here. You were always so strong-willed." Gisela patted Romilly's mousy hair affectionately.

"Gisela." Quilla was stern. "Why is she riding Tycen's horse?"

"Is Tycen. . . the Hisanrial?" Romilly's voice was almost a whisper.

"He must have sent you!" Quilla tried to convince herself that befalling danger had not been part of the equation. Romilly stood and reached to her side, untying the leather bag and handing it to Gisela. Gisela could see now, in the glow of the fire, that she was covered in blood. She swallowed hard.

"Romilly. Where is Tycen? Why have you come?"

Romilly's lip trembled and she wiped away tears with her blood-crusted hands.

"I tried to save him," she cried.

"No!" Quilla shouted and grabbed Romilly in a fistful of robes. "Tell me you're lying!"

"Quill." Gisela gently touched her hand, urging her to release her sister.

"I can see he was beloved." Romilly turned to Quilla and suddenly hugged her, letting her warm tears spill onto Quilla's shoulder. "I promise I tried, but Orien's magic, there was nothing I could do!"

"Orien did this." Quilla clenched her teeth, but she let herself be embraced; it was almost a comfort.

"Tycen tried. . . he tried to kill Orien. We were all watching, but I'm afraid he was no match."

"How did you know to find us?" Gisela wondered.

"His last words were your name Gisela. Your real name. Only Vestals know each other's true names; they're carefully guarded, sacred secrets. Then he gave me this bag. I knew you would have only revealed your name for something very serious. I knew I had to find you and bring it to you." Gisela grabbed the bag and looked at the contents, sighing with relief at the cold, amber bottle inside.

"Thank God for you Romilly!" She squeezed Romilly's hand tightly. "I'm so sorry. For all of us," she said wretchedly. "I'm afraid we have little time to mourn. War is coming to Reliquary, and this prophecy might be our only chance to stop it." Romilly nodded and Quilla looked despondently into the fire.

"I said I'd get you here and back to Rathar safely." Quilla said weakly. "I'm not quittin' now."

Gisela squeezed her shoulder in gratitude. "Romilly, help me prepare to read the prophecy."

The spirit in the forest was both tense and crestfallen. Quilla sat by the fire with her head buried in her lap, peeking between her knees at the two Vestals making their preparations. Romilly had laid her outer garment on the ground, and the two were kneeling before each other, their knees touching with the bottle in Gisela's steady hands. Gisela nodded, began to chant quick, breathy prayers. Quilla stretched her neck out trying to hear them but it was to no avail. They sounded almost like secrets in the dark, but they did not cease for what Quilla thought was ages. She shifted in her seat, stood and gathered wood for the dying fire, but the chanting continued; it must have been hours. Gisela felt the sweat drip down her brow and the aching in her limbs. Romilly tended to her, mopping her brow with a piece of sodden linen, holding her bobbing neck between her hands, and whispering encouragements to her. Then all went quiet. Romilly sat backwards against a log to rest her tired knees, and Gisela nervously... carefully turned out the contents of the amber bottle into her hand; a small scroll of parchment unravelled into her hand and when she gazed upon it, her back suddenly arched unnaturally with a snapping sound. Quilla shrieked wildly as the parchment dissolved in a dazzling blue flame that engulfed Gisela's body.

"No!" Romilly threw herself in front of Quilla. "She is reading." Quilla's eyes were terrified; she suddenly feared the Vestals' secrets.

"What is this magic!?" Quilla wailed.

Just then, Gisela cried out in a voice Quilla had never heard before, almost the scream of a child,

> *"In the face of the ichor two shall be one where*
> *blood is spilt love shall overcome Her sister shall*
> *wield bronze Costly is the castle's arms."*

And then, in an instant the flames extinguished, leaving naught but a trace behind, but Gisela shivering wildly, collapsed on the forest floor. Her eyes were rolling in her head, and she was muttering the words of the prophecy quietly.

"Romilly! What's wrong with her?!"

"We must keep her warm. She'll be okay. She just needs to recover from reading. It takes a lot of strength for a Vestal to read a prophecy." Romilly pulled her garment off of the ground and tucked it around Gisela, rocking and convulsing. Quilla sat beside her and threw her arms over her protectively.

"Sounds ominous." Quilla curled up next to Gisela. Romilly looked off into the darkness toward Reliquary soberly, clutching the empty, amber bottle.

19

ARKYN HAD BROUGHT BACK FOURTEEN Stalkers to the Castle of Borghild; together twenty-one hulking, intimidating figures crowded the great hall of Borghild. They warmed themselves before the ceaseless amethyst flames, poured wine into goblets, shared tales of their ventures and general carousing, and in the center, leaning over the long, oak table, Rathar, Arkyn and Vivica stood with pensive countenances over a large, pleated map of the Provinces. Every now and then one of the Stalkers would belch out an opinion,

"Take 'em head on. Make 'em wish they'd never crossed blades with *us*!"

"You're drunk, you right fool," another would shout, "we're fucked if there are as many aspirmeygs as you all say there are. Suicide mission is what this all is." He pinched his nose and drained his goblet in one swig. "I see the wine is the same mage's sap." He smiled at Vivica, "Right foul, but we'd best get drunk while we still have livers to tarnish!" Some of the Stalkers cheered, but Rathar rolled his eyes, and smoothed out the map again, puffing on the cerise, wooden pipe he often resorted to in times of contemplation.

"They'll approach this way, I'm sure of it. They're soon in full rank with no Stalkers to dwindle their numbers." He ran his finger in a line from the western edge of the Adonican Valley to an inky blotch marked Reliquary. "We'll get there just in time to intercept if we leave by, well, dawn."

"There's no way that magician will have us striding into his city," Arkyn huffed.

"Vivica, what do you have for us?"

Vivica's inky lips twisted into a lovely smile. "Darlings, we may be outnumbered, but we still have the upper hand, of course." She smoothed her dress over the blood-letting wounds on her legs and flinched a little, they still hurt a bit, but she remained in command of her demeanor. "Orien's weakness is his black magic after all. It has its shortcomings, you see. Black magic can only manage one target at a time because its potential is. . . call it flickering. Though it's quite powerful, for it draws on a potent source of potential, that is the wielder, it is wearisome because that potential is liable to run out. Orien's spells can't manage the whole lot of us at once. And as for approaching the city, well," she winked, "we'll go ahead and make sure the way is safe." She pulled Wells by the sleeve of his tunic from a more pleasant conversation he'd been having with two Vestals.

"I say, wait a moment mistress, now wait just a moment." He struggled to free himself from her grip.

"Wells and I will make sure that when you reach Reliquary, Orien is not in your way." She said with a grim flicker in her eyes.

"Mistress," he stammered, "I *am* a magician, this, this is true, but my powers are. . ."

"In working order, I'm sure. We need every man at the ready, Wells. I'll not have you moping about Borghild while others are risking life and limb," she snapped.

"And you'll kill this jester? You do mean to actually slay this son of a bitch, don't you? If you'll have Orien stand trial and answer questions in the courts of your precious Consortium, I'll rightly do it myself," Arkyn snarled.

"Bad blood," Vivica said softly, "is a wicked substitute for sweet wine. It will be his death." There was a savagery in her eyes.

"We're still going to be outnumbered." Arkyn sighed. "The aspirmeygs, Rath, there's too many of them, and what do we do with the girls?" He motioned to the Vestals standing about the room, every one trained in combat and seen her fair share of bloodshed and every one now dependent in the shadow of the coming conflict.

"Let us come," Sabrina came forth courageously, "you *will* need us, Arkyn. The Vestals won't be safe if you start killing. And, we can begin to evacuate my sisters from the city." She was unyielding, and the Stalkers knew that she was right. To begin a fight without their Vestals near could mean innocent bloodshed. Arkyn nodded.

"It's still a losing battle, Rathar. I don't like to say it," he moaned and scratched his whiskers.

"You're forgetting your *faith*, my dears." Vivica grasped their shoulders firmly. "Gisela *will* have arrived in Reliquary by now to retrieve the prophecy. We don't know what it says."

"Do we look to a god for help now?" Rathar looked Vivica hard in the eyes. "We ride at daybreak. I'm inclined to make haste," he hissed. Vivica touched his arm and devoured his thoughts, his anxieties, his regrets. She could feel his pangs so deeply, as if they were her own, and there was a fear in him that was fresh like a new snow that blankets the grass in early harvest. It was a fear that Rathar had never experienced before, the fear of loss, and it afflicted her to see her own so tortured. It was almost a luxury that Stalkers were most often exempt from the aches and misgivings of love and affection; it was an aspect of motherhood that she did not have to traverse: bleeding hearts and melancholy, but then, Rathar had always been different. Vivica squeezed his arm affectionately.

"It is not too late," she whispered. "We have time yet to find her."

•• ———— ••●•• ———— ••

Orien stood from the tall stone turret of the Abbey and looked out onto the Scaenus Plains that flanked the forests bordering Reliquary. They were superbly bucolic, dotted with sheepherder's huts and apple orchards.

"Lovely little spot we've got here." He swirled a silver chalice insouciantly with just his fingertips as the sun set in the window. "Tell me something, Mother, what is *hope*?" The old Abbess lifted her veiled head a bit into the red light of the setting sun.

"It is what drives the very being of every man and woman and child," she said humbly and pulled at the binds on her wrists.

"It is a plague," he said flatly. Mirabelle laughed knowingly from a dark corner of the room where she was sitting on a velvet cushion. "Hope lets people believe that they have power and purpose. That power will lie in *me. Alone.*" Orien bared his teeth at the old Abbess.

"Rathar will come for your army," she said calmly in reply. "He is chosen."

"Stupid old hag. True, I was worried about him when I came to Reliquary for my own prophecy long ago. *The chosen pair stand unpropitious to my sable sorcerer's ambition,*" he recited as if it was affixed in his mind, a verse he played repeatedly, one that tortured his faculties and stole his rest. "But his wretched castle recluse was rightly poisoned and gored—her confidante's guts boil on the roadside, and his precious Vestal is dead. The prophecy is lost; *your hope is lost.* There is nothing to keep him or your legacy safe now, Abbess. Let him come. Let him bring his guttersnipe animals who he calls *family.* They should have been left to die in the mountains, but they will die today; they have no place in my vision, and I will extinguish them, all at once as the opportunity has arisen. My prophecy changes today. The Provinces change today, starting with the Great City."

"Very good, Lord." Mirabelle's words were elongated and untroubled. Mother began to chuckle.

"You will be silent!" Orien dropped his chalice to the floor with an earsplitting ring and curled his fingers bringing the old Abbess to her knees, heaving and vomiting. "I will end the prophecies. I will end your god. I want to see the world bathe in your Vestal blood, old woman. I want to stop the beating heart of all of this pathetic hope. *I will be the one with power,*" he sputtered and with a swift movement of his wrist, he severed the Abbess's spine with a horrendous *crack* leaving her disfigured on the floor.

"Now, was *that* necessary, Orien?" Mirabelle ridiculed, pinching her nose at the smell of the purge on the floor.

"You'll find," two figures emerged from a crackle of amethyst flame and spark, "this pisser no longer decides what's necessary." Vivica's smile was discernable even in the shadow of dusk.

"It is evident why the pigs of Borghild are so ill-mannered." Orien clicked his tongue. "They take after their *mummy*." He pounded his fist on the window ledge. "What is she doing *alive*!?" he bawled.

"Wells." Mirabelle's voice was ardently annoyed. "This *is* the trouble with letting them go rogue." She lifted her hands without moving from her cushion and flicked her fingers forcefully, jetting a curtain of glowing sparks forward. Vivica shielded herself with a quick raise of her forearm and the sparks seemed to melt in midair.

"I think this, this is our fight, Mirabelle." Wells clenched his fist, harnessing the potential of heat in the room from body and breath, and shot a burst of flame so near her face it singed the hair curled neatly at her ear.

"Very well," she said darkly. "You want to play with fire. We'll play with fire." Mirabelle closed her eyes and mumbled an incantation, exhaling hot breath that sparked wildly in her hands, and before they knew it, the whole turret was up in roaring flame, tapestries and arrases, scrolls, cushions, anything flammable was ablaze with wild heat and conflagration. Vivica looked around bewildered,

"Orien is gone!" she shouted above the tumult.

"Go." Wells gritted his teeth, casting a curse towards Mirabelle, diving for the cover of a crumbling wall. "I'll, I'll take care of her!" Vivica marveled at Wells's newfound courage, but she had no time for revelations; she had to keep Orien distracted, and better yet dead, if she could find him.

Meanwhile the fire had spread from the turret to the great Abbey and was now unfurling across the countless trees on the grounds of Reliquary like a disease spreading in a dirty drum. As Vestals began to flood toward the gates of the city making for the bordering forest which opened out onto the plains for escape, a Vestal, out of breath, came running toward the gate.

"Wait!" she cried. "Wait! We can't leave!"

"What do you mean, we can't leave?! The city is on fire, Tufi!"

"I've just come from the towers! Aspirmeygs! They're. . . Oh God, they're marching toward the city. . . like an army! In lines!"

"It's Orien! He did this! Where is Mother?" another cried.

"We have to make for the arsenal! It's underground," Tufi gasped. "Take the children and run!" The Vestals stood and looked at each other, leaderless and did not know what they should do.

"Do what she says." A Vestal came forward holding two children in wheaten robes by the hand. "Tufi is meant to be paired with a Stalker. She knows more about surviving than any of you scholars or clergy girls. *Do what she says.*" The Vestals, running through the burning city, choking on smoke, filed into the arsenal and huddled together, warm bodies imbricated with cold bronze blades, filling it to the brim. Tufi shut the heavy iron door to keep out the smoke, the growing heat, and the impending foes. They could do nothing but wait while they listened to the foul shrieking in the distance growing nearer, becoming deafening.

"How many are there?" cried one Vestal.

"More than a hundred," another replied in awe. The shrieks and screeches grew closer until the Vestals were covering their ears.

"They're looking for us! They have to be!" one sobbed.

"How can anything survive out there in that fire?"

"Only a Stalker's blade could help us now!"

"They're going to murder us!"

"Stop it, all of you," Tufi commanded. "You're scaring the children. We must be brave." She squeezed her eyes tightly as the screeches and squeals of aspirmeygs cascaded onto her beloved Reliquary. "We must be brave for God and for each other," she whispered.

Chapter

20

T HIS WAS NOT THE RELIQUARY Rathar knew.
He remembered the billowing, green trees and stone
fountains, the archways and long, stretching lawns. He
remembered sitting in the Abbey, pulling the loose threads on
the cushion of his seat lazily on a sultry summer afternoon as the
Abbess had spoken to him about his duty to protect this Vestal
as a servant and representative of God. He remembered looking
out into a sea of wheaten robes begrudgingly wondering which
one he'd have to drag along with him. He remembered the smell
of incense and the taste of bland tea. But now he smelled thick
smoke and saw a city in flames against the night sky, flooded with
aspirmeygs. Maybe she was in there, somewhere. His hope was
wavering, but it was still flickering somewhere inside him like a
candle near extinguished.

"Stick to the plan! Arkyn takes the Vestals to find their sisters. The rest of us slaughter as many of these beasts as possible!" The Stalkers gave a thundering shout. Slowly, they began to shift, and it would have been hideous for anyone to behold. It was like a plague creeping over them one by one. Scarlet bruises smirching their ashen skin and bulky, tendrils of tangled tissue covering their eyes. They were restless with murderous hunger, and rode headlong into the city, blades drawn.

•• ———— ••●•• ———— ••

Rathar frowned as a bead of sweat trickled down his face. He told himself that it was the boiling heat of the burning city around him, but these enchanted aspirmeygs were stubborn to die. He hacked wildly against the neck of a Notos whose icy claw threatened to pin him to the ground and purple blood sprayed forth. *Five.* He tallied in his mind and smiled viciously.

•• ———— ••●•• ———— ••

"Romilly, look!" Quilla pointed at the rising smoke in the distance. "Reliquary is on fire!" She looked down at Gisela wrapped up on the saddle in front of her; she had been too weak to ride on her own.

"My sisters," Romilly pleaded, "we have to go!" Quilla nodded and adjusted Gisela in the saddle, winding her own legs under Sela's to make sure she stayed upright, and then reached out toward Romilly. "I don't know what we'll find when we get there. But your duty is to your sisters now. Don't look back for nothin', Romilly. Just keep going." She nodded and they took off at a gallop through the forest toward Reliquary.

When they arrived, the scene was devastating. The fire had spread to every corner of the city, no place was left untouched. Stalkers were brawling with aspirmeygs in hordes though they were greatly outnumbered; some slain bodies of the champions of Borghild, overcome by the sheer number of enemies, were already strewn about the ground.

"Sabrina!" Romilly shouted. "Sabrina, where are the others?!" She and Quilla rode up to a group of Vestals being protected, though safety seemed waning, by a single Stalker. The chaos around them was encroaching. Arkyn slashed mightily and cost an Eurus his wriggling arm before putting all his weight into a swing that left the beast's head rolling before Romilly's horse. He was breathing heavily.

"We're looking for them now! They may have escaped!"

"No." Romilly put her hand to her lips in thought.

"Think faster, girls." Arkyn charged at another aspirmeyg making its way toward the Vestals with a hungry screech. "I don't have all fucking night!"

"The arsenal." Romilly said decidedly. "It's the only place safe from fire."

"Wait!" Quilla shouted, struggling to hold Gisela up in the saddle still. "I *need* to find Rathar."

"The chosen pair." Sabrina nodded. "This way. Then to the arsenal. It's no use finding our sisters if we can't stop these beasts."

"Fine with me!" Arkyn laughed ravenously and slashed and sliced his way through the burning city.

•• ——— ••●•• ——— ••

Rathar's heart dropped like a stone. He thought, for a moment, it stopped beating, and he felt in his body something of an unnatural reaction. He was beginning to shift back, a completely emotional response. *Shit* he thought as the corded flesh over his eyes began to recede slowly. What was happening? But it was no mistake, he could smell her. It was her figure approaching, slumped over a saddle, vulnerable, hurting. He was confused and disoriented, and his body chemistry was turbulent. He grappled almost involuntarily with the aspirmeyg he had kicked against the wall before him, plunging his hand into its gorget and tearing its throat out with his fist. It fell to the ground in a puddle of purple before he turned around at the approaching group.

"Gisela!" He winced and tried desperately to cling to his body's superior adaptations, but they were dissolving at a rapid rate with a ubiquitous pain moreover. "What's wrong with her? Quilla, what's wrong with her!?"

"She read the prophecy, Rathar, she's recovering. It might. . . it might take a while." He hadn't realized he'd been holding his breath, now relieved, he gasped for air. "*In the face of the ichor two shall be one, where blood is spilt love shall overcome, Her sister shall wield bronze, Costly is the castle's arms.* That's what it said." Quilla looked from Rathar to Gisela desperately. He squeezed his eyes together for a moment, blinking through the smoke.

"Did you find the other Vestals?" he said gravely clenching the hilt of his sword with white knuckles.

"We think they're in the arsenal." Arkyn kicked aside the head of an unlucky Stalker, a fearsome grimace still on his face. "And I'd say we're running out of time for your *faith* and riddles." When they arrived at the arsenal, the door was too hot for the Vestals to open it from the inside. Arkyn and Rathar advised the Vestals to stand back and kicked the door down like nothing more than a boyhood contest. They arrived to a sea of tawny robes and mixed faces. Some were terrified, sure they'd be dead before morning. Some were brave and mulish, those were the ones Rathar needed to rally most. He gently laid Gisela in the midst of the crowd.

"You don't know me." He tried to swallow his savagery like bitter medicine.

"You're Rathar of Borghild. You're the chosen pair!" Tufi shouted out.

"Okay, you do know me." He scratched the back of his neck, slightly embarrassed. Arkyn would have rolled his eyes if he could have.

"*In the face of the ichor two shall be one, where blood is spilt love shall overcome, Her sister shall wield bronze, Costly is the castle's arms.* . . I don't think I'm the only one who knows what that means."

"No, you're definitely the only one who knows what that means," Arkyn said, dumbfounded.

"It means we have an army bigger than we thought we had. See Gisela and I. . . we. . . we're in. . . I. . . suffice it to say, I can share my Stalker's powers with her." There was some general chatter and awe among the Vestals. "And because you're all Vestals you're. . ."

"We're connected on the spiritual plane," Sabrina said affirmatively. "What you share with her, you can share with any of us. All of us. At the same time, theoretically."

"The prophecy says. . . it'll be at great cost," one Vestal said, petrified.

"Look around you," Tufi cried, "this *is* at great cost!"

"We don't know how to use swords," another one said humbly.

"Just swing the damned things. Better an army of you than the few of us that're left." Arkyn coughed some black soot onto his sleeve. "If ya can't reach their necks, go for the bellies or the knees till you can reach what's *necessary*." Tufi nodded and one by one Vestals started standing in agreement, picking up bronze blades from the arsenal walls. "Ya hold it like this." Arkyn demonstrated. "And swing like this." He swished his own blade through the air. "Now do it, Rath, our men are out there getting swatted like flies."

Rathar closed his eyes and was sitting by a small brook. He inhaled deep through his nose, Lily of the Valley. He pricked up his ears and heard something familiar, the dulcet laugh of Gisela sitting next to him, her voice was always as sweet as a song. *Don't go*, he called out as her face faded next to him. *Does it please you?* Her song echoed and her grey eyes vanished, crushing his heart into mangled pain he'd only felt once before, the day she really left him; the day he knew he loved her.

"Take it," he said forcefully and opened his eyes to the sight of hundreds of shifted Vestals before him. "Fight for yourselves." He urged them onwards, and they poured out of the arsenal into the smoldering city. "Wait here for me, Quilla, please." He tucked Gisela against the arsenal wall. "I'll come back for you." He kissed Gisela's head and ran out into the blaze once more.

•• —————— ••●•• —————— ••

Mirabelle was panting and out of breath. She continued to shove pulses of jet-black energy at Wells, drawing potential from the only source her forbidden magic could reap from—*herself*, but he was lighter on his feet.

"That's the thing about your black magic. . ." Wells raised his brow and cast a spell of bright blue light from a cluster of bluebell blossoms crumpled in his fist knocking the magician off her feet. She landed hard on her back and her heart began to palpitate rapidly. Mirabelle clutched her chest and grimaced. "It taxes you." The spell had rendered Mirabelle inert. "Shame, I've got a marvelous herbal tonic for that."

"What will *you* do, apothecary? Kill me?" she gasped. "The Consortium would have your head."

"I'm afraid, I, I already have yours." Wells reached down and grasped Mirabelle's head betwixt his hands and with a sudden jerk, snapped her neck and left her limp on the floor amid the fire and the ashes. He pursed his lips unpleasantly at the sound. *"I'll not have you moping about Borghild while others are risking life and limb.* Well how's that for moping about?" Wells mocked Vivica. "Blazes, Wellsburg! This place is going up in blazes!" he shouted and made for the stairs.

•• ———— ••●•• ———— ••

Gisela awoke with a shudder to the horrible sound of shrieking, roaring, and painful death. She looked around and in her own time realized where she was. "Quilla?" she called out.

"Sela! Here I am!" Quilla scrambled in front of Gisela. "How are you feeling?! You've been asleep for days!"

"Quilla how did we get here? What's going on out there? Why is it so. . . why is it so hot?" She shifted uncomfortably and yanked off the outer garment of her Vestal's robes.

"Sela. . . promise me you'll stay right here with me. Promise. You're in no condition to go out there. And my God, he'd kill me, he really would. . . especially in his present state of mind."

"Who? Rathar? Was Rathar here?" Gisela leapt to her feet, though a bit uneasy, and she swayed.

"I told him the prophecy, Sela; he made all the Vestals into Stalkers. All of 'em!" She threw her arms over her head. But all we can do. . . is wait, Gisela. He said he'd come back for us."

"I'm tired of being useless to him." Over Gisela's arms pink and red marks began to rise, then slowly up her neck.

"No way!" Quilla grabbed her arm, but Gisela easily threw her off and unsheathed her bronze blade. She ran out of the arsenal with Quilla close behind. "I can't leave you!" Quilla shouted. "I promised!" As they weaved through the paths, Gisela felt sick. The bodies of her sisters littered the streets, everywhere she looked was absolute carnage, and the ones who were still standing, still fighting didn't look like they had a chance for long. Her own senses were deteriorated from her present condition; she didn't notice the massive Zephyr come around the corner of the disintegrating stone wall of the Abbey, and she nearly ran right into its hulking canine body hunched over on the prowl. She swung as hard as she could, aiming for its jugular, but missed, and it yowled in provocation. She steadied herself and tried again, swinging for its massive paw, but she was dizzy and her miscalculation and the weight of her own flourish brought her hard to the ground. Suddenly, she let out a piercing scream. Agony ripped through her as if she was being taken by a river's swift current. The Zephyr had swung his whetted claws and cut both of Gisela's legs clean off. She sat aghast, bleeding, screaming. The Zephyr came lunging at her for its final quell, when from behind the beast a blade plunged through its wisping bosom. Arkyn cracked through the spine with a crazed shout of ecstasy and whipped his sword through the air, daring another to come near.

"I'm still alive!" He laughed wildly. "But you won't be, lass, if you don't get on this horse." He picked Quilla up by a handful of tunic and pulled her over the saddle.

"Stop! We can't leave her! I can't leave her!"

"Just another loss, lass. We've got to move on." He kicked the horse's sides and took off through the city, Quilla's screams echoing through the cascading walls. Gisela began to tear her robes and tie the bloody stumps of her legs with the scraps. The pain was searing, and she had never felt more helpless. She saw in the distance where a falling piece of stone had made a small crevice where she could be well concealed, and she began to crawl for safety.

•• ———— ••●•• ———— ••

Vivica bolted through the corridors of the Abbey, congested and choking on the smoke that hung in the air. The thought of finding Orien consumed her as she beat down doors buckled shut from the heat. Her legs were aching from the prominent scores that embellished them. *Her legs.*

"I need Rathar," she hissed. "He's probably the only Stalker here not in such a frenzy as to think." Vivica raced down to the main doors of the Abbey and looked out into the streets. The carnage was ghastly. Her own sons lay mutilated at her feet as she ducked through the tumbling stone and skirmishes screaming Rathar's name.

"Vivica, I'm here," Rathar called, slicing the head clean off a Eurus in a wisping torrent.

"Together we must face Orien, Rathar." Vivica ducked out of the way as Rathar cleaved his sword into the skull of an unsuspecting Boreas that had backed into the alleyway beside them. "The only way to beat Orien at his own game is with his own game, but I haven't enough potential since my last exploits, and I won't be able to get a clean cut at him for certain; I need *you*, Rathar." Rathar nodded grimly. He knew of the talents of the Mistress of Borghild; her magic was no secret to her brood.

"Is that not him, there on the turret like a peacock?" Rathar pointed his sword to a figure cloaked in black furs standing atop the tallest turret overlooking the ruin.

"We must be swift." Vivica looked down at a lifeless, bloodied body that rolled across her feet she once raised as Dag and kissed his cinder-soiled cheek. The turret was built into the side of a large church, and aspirmeygs had already begun to rip through it.

"That staircase suddenly seems a long way away." Rathar inhaled sharply, calculating how many to one of the slinking figures ravaging the holy building and its relics there were.

"Clearly they have an agenda," Vivica murmured.

"We'll clear your way." Tufi stepped confidently onto the stoop of the church with a band of Vestals behind her. "For our God!" she cried and whipped her sword in front of her, leading her sisters into the church. They gashed and tore at the aspirmeygs, bellies, necks if they could reach them, and all places tender, with fearsome cries for meek and humble churchwomen, clearing a path for Rathar and Vivica to make it to the stair to the turret. When they neared the top, Vivica pulled Rathar aside with a whisper.

"My darling, do you remember when you were a boy? And I would prick your finger with a pin?" Vivica cooed and touched Rathar's cheek.

"To show me my own potential. What was capable inside of me. You would drop it on the dormant mosses and make them come awake, then with another drop you would deaden them once more."

"Think of what two can do."

"*Where blood is spilt, love shall overcome,*" he rasped.

•• ———— ••●•• ———— ••

"*This* is the prophecy I feared? An army of clerics who can barely wield their swords?" Orien chuckled from the top of the turret.

"Stop running." Vivica tumbled out from the top of the tower stair onto the naked pinnacle.

"I simply wanted a view." Orien swept his arm across the city in ruin.

"Of genocide?" Vivica riposted.

"I won't explain again what I had to explain to that dreary Abbess. It's necessary. Look at that fool's army, it's all going to death. He's practically doing it for me." He smiled, and Vivica winced at the bodies, like flotsam washed up on shore for miles. Piles of them, burning, lying in the grit, Stalkers and Vestals alike, some no older than children. They were losing badly.

"Orien," she took a daring step closer to him, "you must stop this. This magic is beneath you."

"No. The Consortium is beneath me. What it was. What it could never be. I am a metamorphosis." He turned to face Vivica with cruelty in his expression. "What would a hermitess who hides in the bogs, using her magic to turn babies into rabid dogs know of *my magic*. You think I need magic to kill you, you backwards bitch?" Orien instantaneously pulled from his belt a small knife, typically used for augury, and drove it into her clenched stomach. She smiled, and the grimace slowly faded from his face.

"I know something of your magic." She wiped her hand across the wound in her stomach and then pressed it against his forehead.

"B. . . blood magic." He quaked.

"Rath!" she called, and Rathar emerged from the shadows onto the turret apogee. He placed his hand, streaming with blood next to Vivica's on top of Orien's forehead, lending his potential to the rune. She closed her eyes and muttered a dark incantation before clenching her fist tightly, and before her eyes, Orien erupted from the inside out, squelched in a pile of entrails, blood, and splintered bone.

"At least it's not on my floor this time." Vivica sighed and held the knife tightly to her abdomen, not daring to let it release. Looking out from the tower, she saw the remaining aspirmeygs suddenly slump to the ground, totally lifeless, all magic and viability siphoned out of them. The battle, at great cost, was over. She stepped over Orien's lifeless body. "You've done it." She took her free hand and caressed Rathar's perspiring brow. "Good boy." She groaned in pain and held her hand to her abdomen where a faint glow of silver began to halt the bleeding. They descended the tower together. The handful of Stalkers and Vestals that endured looked on amazed, and relieved, as their adversaries fell before them.

"Come!" Vivica was riding through the city gathering up the still living remnants she could find. "The city is collapsing! 'Tis not safe to remain any longer! We make for Borghild!"

"I have to go back to the arsenal!" Rathar ran up to Vivica. "I have to go back for—"

"Rathar!" Quilla was shrieking wildly despite the choking smoke.

"This one won't shut her gob!" Arkyn was exasperated. "I'd rip her pining heart out if naught for these Vestals." He gritted his teeth.

"Gisela! She's somewhere! She's out there! She's hurt badly! I'm so sorry!" Quilla was sobbing and grasping for Rathar, but Arkyn kept her firmly on the saddle.

"Take them on, Vivica, Arkyn. Lead them to the castle."

"It's no use, Rathar. She's as good as gone out there," Arkyn scoffed.

Rathar growled a low, wrathful growl and snapped back, "You heard what I said. Get everyone out. I'm *going* to find her."

"Save your arse when it comes down to it." Arkyn kicked his horse and began to lead the ragged band of survivors out of the city.

"You've shifted back entirely, Rathar; you don't have the strength to remain." Vivica urged. "Promise me you'll make for Borghild if you do not find her *soon*." Rathar grunted, and Vivica nodded sadly, watching Rathar run off into the smoke and falling stone.

•• ——— ••●•• ——— ••

Rathar's heart beat wildly in an anxiety that crushed him and reduced him to quivers and panting. He raced through the city, climbing over fallen stone and corses piled in the streets. He was so hot that he was sodden through his tunic with sweat, choking on mouthfuls of ash. He tried to hone his senses, but the smoke was too thick to pick up her all too familiar scent. *Promise me you'll make for Borghild if you do not find her soon. It's not too late. We have time yet to find her.* Rathar made two white knuckled fists and wailed into the night.

•• ——— ••●•• ——— ••

Gisela could hardly feel her legs anymore, or rather, where they used to be, but she could see them lying in the bloody, gravel path where she'd crawled from. Maybe it was the racing in her heart. Maybe it was her Stalker's powers. She dared not begin to shift back, just in case, but she no longer heard the shrieks and squeals of aspirmeygs. She also no longer heard the screams and moans of her sisters dying. All she heard was the low rumble and crackle of flames and falling stone. It was so hot she wanted to rip off her robes. Though she could not hear the sounds of terror any longer, she still feared to crawl out of her hiding place, so she remained, tucked away, longing. She longed for earthen hair and strong arms to find her, to pick her up and carry her somewhere safe. She longed to apologise; *I'm sorry I ever left you. I'm sorry I brought this destruction on my sisters. I'm sorry we were the chosen pair. I'm sorry I couldn't be just a Vestal to you. Are you alive, Rath? Are you out there?* Tears began to sting her purple and ash-stained face. She felt dizzy. She closed her eyes, just for a moment, and she thought she could smell something other than smoke. Yes, something sweet.

A posy. Winter heather. Lily of the Valley. Snowdrops. It was just a dream.

"Do they please you?" she whispered. *"They please me very much."* She smiled as her blood drained and her head spun.

ACKNOWLEDGMENTS

Thank you first and foremostly to Emma for the time and effort poured into helping me make this book what it is today. Thank you for the enthusiasm and the heart that helps make me feel like what I have written is worth something.

Thank you Star and Emir for helping me bring my artistic vision to life in your own ways.

Thank you Evangeline and Lisa for making me feel informed and secure throughout the entire process of a debut novel. I appreciate your enthusiasm and support.

Thank you to Angie for your hours of work and willingness to compromise and teach. You helped make this book what it needed to be, and I am forever grateful.

Thank you to everyone who truly was excited about this project and waited patiently for the fruit of my labour. You inspire me as an author.

ABOUT RIZE PRESS

RIZE publishes great stories and great writing across genres written by People of Color and other underrepresented groups. Our team consists of:

Lisa Diane Kastner, Founder and Executive Editor

Joelle Mitchell, Licensing and Strategy Lead

Cody Sisco, Acquisition Editor, RIZE

Benjamin White, Acquisition Editor, Running Wild

Peter A. Wright, Acquisition Editor, Running Wild

Resa Alboher, Editor

Angela Andrews, Editor

Sandra Bush, Editor

Ashley Crantas, Editor

Rebecca Dimyan, Editor

Abigail Efird, Editor

Aimee Hardy, Editor

Henry L. Herz, Editor

Cecilia Kennedy, Editor

Barbara Lockwood, Editor

AE Williams, Editor

Scott Schultz, Editor

Rod Gilley, Editor

Kelly Ottiano, Editor

Carolyn Banks, Editor

Evangeline Estropia, Product Manager

Pulp Art Studios, Cover Design

Standout Books, Interior Design

Polgarus Studios, Interior Design

Learn more about us and our stories at
www.runningwildpublishing.com

Loved this story and want more? Follow us at
www.runningwildpublishing.com/rize,
www.facebook.com/runningwildpress,
on Twitter @lisadkastner @RunWildBooks @RwpRIZE

RUNNING WILD

RIZE